Marry Jessie. She Wants A Baby, You Want A Family.

The idea was so shocking that Ryan stopped dead in the middle of the sidewalk, causing a woman to glance at him oddly.

Marry Jessie. The thought made his heart race alarmingly. Part of him was still that adolescent boy with a crush on his lissome young neighbor. With those long legs and the graceful way she carried herself, she was most definitely elegant, but she was also volatile. If she disagreed with him, she said so in no uncertain terms.

He'd told himself he was over Jessie, that she'd been an adolescent fantasy. But in the back of his mind he knew he'd been comparing other women to her for the past ten years or more.

And he *was* over her. Just because he couldn't stop thinking about her didn't mean anything except that he was still as physically attracted to her as he'd always been.

Was it ridiculous to think that he could make a life with her now, a life that included the children he'd always wanted?

He reached for the phone. After all, what did he have to lose?

Dear Reader,

Ring in the New Year with the hottest new love stories from Silhouette Desire! *The Redemption of Jefferson Cade* by BJ James is our MAN OF THE MONTH. In this latest installment of MEN OF BELLE TERRE, the youngest Cade overcomes both external and internal obstacles to regain his lost love. And be sure to read the launch book in Desire's first yearlong continuity series, DYNASTIES: THE CONNELLYS. In *Tall, Dark & Royal*, bestselling author Leanne Banks introduces a prominent Chicago family linked to European royals.

Anne Marie Winston offers another winner with *Billionaire Bachelors: Ryan*, a BABY BANK story featuring twin babies. In *The Tycoon's Temptation* by Katherine Garbera, a jaded billionaire discovers the greater rewards of love, while Kristi Gold's *Dr. Dangerous* discovers he's addicted to a certain physical therapist's personal approach to healing in this launch book of Kristi's MARRYING AN M.D. miniseries. And Metsy Hingle bring us *Navy SEAL Dad*, a BACHELORS & BABIES story.

Start the year off right by savoring all six of these passionate, powerful and provocative romances from Silhouette Desire!

Enjoy!

Joan Marlow Golan

Joan Marlow Golan
Senior Editor, Silhouette Desire

Please address questions and book requests to:
Silhouette Reader Service
U.S.: 3010 Walden Ave., P.O. Box 1325, Buffalo, NY 14269
Canadian: P.O. Box 609, Fort Erie, Ont. L2A 5X3

Billionaire
Bachelors: Ryan
ANNE MARIE WINSTON

Published by Silhouette Books
America's Publisher of Contemporary Romance

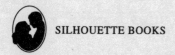 **SILHOUETTE BOOKS**

ISBN 0-373-76413-8

BILLIONAIRE BACHELORS: RYAN

Copyright © 2002 by Anne Marie Rodgers

Visit Silhouette at www.eHarlequin.com

Printed in U.S.A.

ANNE MARIE WINSTON

RITA Award finalist and bestselling author Anne Marie Winston loves babies she can give back when they cry, animals in all shapes and sizes and just about anything that blooms. When she's not writing, she's chauffeuring children to various activities, trying *not* to eat chocolate or reading anything she can find. She will dance at the slightest provocation and weeds her gardens when she can't see the sun for the weeds anymore. You can learn more about Anne Marie's novels by visiting her Web site at www.annemariewinston.com.

For Mary Anne Trent

"Truly great friends are hard to find,
difficult to leave, and impossible to forget."
—G. Randolf

Jessie Reilly was still chortling as she dropped the magazine back into her bag. "I'm impressed," she said, and the sparkle dancing in her eyes made him narrow his own. They'd grown up together and he knew that look. It usually meant trouble for him. "I mean, who'd ever have thought that skinny kid next door would grow up to be an 'eminently available hunk'?"

Ryan forgot to be annoyed as her amused gaze met his. Jessie looked as good as she always did to him, in a slim-fitting charcoal suit and high black boots to protect her feet from January's icy weather, and he felt the familiar little shock of attraction in his solar plexus when her wide smile lit her face. "If I'd known you were bringing that rag," he told her, "I might have skipped lunch." *Right. Like you'd ever miss an opportunity to spend time with Jessie.*

Jessie had been his neighbor during his childhood, his first hopeless adolescent love and his good friend forever. She joined him here on the third Wednesday of every month for lunch. As she shook her dark hair back from her face, it gleamed with coppery highlights. He was aware that more than one man in the room watched her as she relaxed at the table he'd reserved by the fireplace in the Ritz-Carlton Hotel's bar.

"I'm glad you didn't skip out on me," she told him. "I've been thinking about you, wondering how you're doing." Her eyes were a smoky green-gray in the winter light streaming through the windows that overlooked the Public Garden, a dark ring around the irises giving them a striking intensity. He knew she didn't just want to know generally how life was. She meant, "How are you getting along since Wendy's death?" She'd asked him the same question, casually sandwiched into their conversations, once a month for the past two years. But he didn't want to go there today, so he answered it in the general sense.

"Life's good. Business is good. How about you?"

Her eyes reproached him but she let it slide. "I'm all right. Business is...business."

Something in her tone made him glance sharply at her, and to his critical eye her expression looked troubled. "Something wrong at the gallery?"

"Not wrong, exactly." She hesitated. "I just learned this morning that my biggest rival in the area is expanding. Until now they haven't affected my business at all, but with a larger place and more inventory..." She shrugged. "It's a little worrisome."

Jessie owned a fine arts gallery a block away on Newbury Street that catered to the idle rich and those who aspired to the lifestyle. Ryan had bought gifts there in the past and he'd been impressed by both the quality and the unique selection of items she stocked. The prices...she clearly had targeted the well-to-do doctors and lawyers that blanketed the Boston population like the snow outside the windows covered the landscape. "So what are you going to do about it?"

"I don't know." Their drinks arrived, and she curled long, delicate fingers around the stem of her wineglass. "I've barely had time to think at all this morning. It was busy from the moment the doors opened until I sneaked out at lunch time." Then she shrugged her shoulders, deliberately shaking off her cares. "I'll figure something out, I'm sure."

"I'm sure you will." He toasted her with his drink. "You're one of the most resourceful people I know. Not to mention bullheaded, stubborn and tenacious."

She shot him a narrow-eyed stare. "Gee, thanks. I think." She took a sip of her drink.

The waitress approached and he ordered lobster sandwiches for each of them. They made small talk until their meals arrived, discussing the lousy—if expected—winter weather, a new artisan Jessie had discovered who hand wove silk scarves and blankets, a new idea he was kicking around.

Minutes later a shadow fell across the table. He glanced up, expecting food. Instead, a tall blonde with enormous blue eyes stood beside the table. She looked like she might be twenty-one. Maybe.

"Ryan Shaughnessy?" The voice was low, smoky, calculated to arouse.

"That's me. And this is Jessie Reilly."

Jessie started to offer her hand but the blonde merely flicked her one disinterested glance and then turned back to Ryan, giving him her hand as if she expected it to be kissed. "Hello. I'm Amalia Hunt. Of the Beacon Hill Hunts? Would you like to join me for dinner? Tonight, if you're available, or any night of your choosing."

Good God. Not again. He sighed and released her hand. "Miss Hunt. Of the Beacon Hill Hunts." It was hard to keep the sarcasm suppressed. The elite of Boston's elite were a truly unique species. Very taken with their own status and too insular to recognize that said status wasn't worth much in the real world. He sighed again. "Thank you for your kind offer, but I'm afraid I'll have to decline." He tilted his head meaningfully at Jessie.

The young woman's eyes flicked over Jessie again, probably estimating her net worth based on her wardrobe and jewelry. "My loss. But if you change your mind, here's my card." She leaned forward and tucked a business card into the breast pocket of his suit jacket, giving him a truly enjoyable view down the front of her low-cut blouse as she did so. "Bye-bye."

Jessie coughed, and he realized she was on the verge of choking with laughter. He glowered at her. Well, hell, he wasn't going to go out with Miss Beacon Hill, but he was a man, wasn't he?

The young woman drifted away, leaving dead silence in her wake.

"Don't say a word." Ryan looked across the table at Jessie. She was looking down at her linked hands again, but he knew it was only because she was trying not to burst into laughter. "Not…a…word," he repeated through his teeth.

The server appeared with their meals then, saving him for the moment.

When the man departed, Jessie said, "Well, gee, considering you used me as an excuse to brush off that poor little thing…"

"You were convenient," he said. "On the way here I got stopped by a woman with a similar proposition. I could have used you then, too."

Jessie grinned. "Such a cross to bear."

He ignored her needling as he applied himself to his meal. Lobster sandwiches were a house specialty, and they dug in.

Well, he dug in. Jess was a nibbler. She could make a meal last longer than it took a Southerner to recite the Declaration of Independence. When his sandwich was gone, he looked hopefully across at hers. She was still nibbling one section, but when she caught him eyeing the other half, she put a protective hand over it and said, "No way, José."

She knew him too well. "Never hurts to try."

When he looked back at Jessie, she was chewing her lower lip and her face looked troubled. Something was bugging her. Or she was thinking about something important. But given the way she was scrunching up her brow, he suspected a problem.

He and Jessie had grown up next door to each other in Charlestown, north of Boston across the Inner Harbor, squarely in the center of the blue-collar Irish district. That had been two decades before the first waves of young urban professionals had discovered the pretty, bow-fronted houses. His father had been a stonemason. She'd lived with her grandparents and her mother, who'd worked two jobs most of her life.

Jessie was two years younger than he. She'd been his first love. No, it had been infatuation, even if it had lasted an inordinately long time, he assured himself. And it hadn't been returned. As far as he knew, she'd never known how he felt about her when they'd been teenagers. It was probably a good thing. He treasured the friendship they still shared.

"You've got something on your mind," he said, resisting the urge to reach over and smooth the furrows from her forehead with his thumb.

It was an educated guess, but her eyes widened, and an odd look—consternation mixed with something that looked almost defiant—crossed her face. She nodded. "I do. I wanted to talk with you about a decision I'm considering."

"Why me?"

She eyed him cautiously. "Because you're my oldest friend and you probably know me better than anybody in the world and I need an honest opinion." She didn't pause for a single breath throughout the recitation.

He picked up his wine and took a sip, savoring the light, crisp taste of the vintage. "All right. What's up?"

"I'm thinking about having a baby."

He heard the words, but it was as if they hit an invisible

wall and bounced off. He shook his head slowly, trying to wrap his brain around the syllables and turn them into something sensible. *I'm thinking about having a baby.* Nope. They still didn't want to compute. Hell, he'd expected her to bring up something to do with her business. Something for which she needed his financial wisdom.

Carefully, not meeting her eyes, he said, "I wasn't aware you were...with anyone."

"I'm not."

Thank God. The reaction was immediate and instinctive, relief rushing through him so heavily he felt as if he might sag beneath its weight.

It was only that he felt protective toward her, he assured himself. Nothing more. Well, at least, nothing more than serious fondness. He'd loved her wildly, futilely, through his high school years, had pined for her during college when she'd been with someone else, had finally recognized his obsession, conquered it and married a wonderful woman. Jessie and Wendy had been friends from the day they'd met, as well. Wendy had joined them at these lunches often in what he thought of now as "the old days." It was only natural that he would still feel some attachment to Jessie. She was a large part of his past.

"Ryan?" Her voice called him back to the present. "Are you all right? I didn't mean to give you such a shock."

Slowly he shook his head to clear it. "If you're not in a relationship, then how do you propose to, ah, get started on a baby?"

"That's what a cryobank is for."

"A cryobank?" He knew what she meant but he couldn't believe what he was hearing.

Color rose in her cheeks and she didn't meet his eyes. "It's a sperm freezing and storage facility." She reached into her satchel again as she spoke. "I've already been through a battery of tests at a fertility center. I've had some preliminary testing and a physical. They started me on some special vitamins and things. I'm considered an excellent candidate for pregnancy. All I have to do is select a donor and have the procedure done."

"The procedure?"

"Artificial insemination." She came up for air with a folder clutched in her hand. "I've already selected some possibilities but I wanted your opinion." She extended the folder across the table.

Ryan stared at it, making no move to take it. "Tell me you're not serious."

Jessie's gaze was level. She didn't speak.

"Oh, hell." He rested his elbows on the table and speared the fingers of both hands through his hair. "You *are* serious. Jess…why? Why this way? Why right now?"

"I'm going to be thirty in November, Ryan." Her voice was quiet. All traces of the earlier humor had fled. "I want a family. Children," she amended. "I want to be a parent while I'm still young and energetic enough to keep up with my kids and enjoy them." Unspoken between them was the memory of her own childhood, one that he knew had been lonely and joyless. He remembered her grandparents as stuffy, disapproving old prunes who had never forgiven their only daughter for an out-of-wedlock pregnancy. And Jessie's mother…well, the best thing his own mother, who rarely had a harsh word to say about anyone, had said was, "It wouldn't kill her to cuddle that little girl once in a while."

"Thirty is young," he said desperately. "Women are having children well into their forties these days. Why don't you wait just a few more years? You might feel totally differently—"

"I didn't ask you to criticize me," she said sharply, and he could see the rising Irish temper that went with the red glints in her hair. "I've already decided to have a baby. I merely wanted your opinion on which donor I should choose. But just forget it." She started to withdraw the folder, but he grabbed it from her.

"Wait." He was stalling, trying to think of some way to talk her out of this insane idea. The thought of Jessie, *his* Jessie, going to a sperm bank, caused his chest to grow tight with repugnance. "I'll look at them."

He placed the folder in front of him, looking down over the list of information contained on the first set of stapled sheets, then scanning the second and the third. There were at least three more. "These don't provide a lot of information."

"Oh, these are just the preliminary profiles," she said. "If I like some of these, I'll request medical and personal profiles that are much more detailed. Family background, academic records, that sort of thing."

"Who fills these out?"

"There are medical evaluations and personality test, things like that," she said, "but most of the personal information comes from the…the donors." She looked past him rather than at him.

"And does anyone check to see if they're telling the truth?"

"I…well…I don't know." Her eyebrows rose. "Why would they lie?"

"Beats me. But to assume that the information these anonymous men volunteer is accurate…isn't that a pretty big risk? I read a case about a guy who knew he carried a rare genetic heart defect that often resulted in death during the young adult years—and he lied on his application. Later, he had an attack of guilt and told his genetics counselor, but when they contacted the sperm bank, his sperm already had produced successful pregnancies for several women. It was a big bioethical mess.''

Jessie rubbed her temples with her hands. ''That has to be a pretty isolated incident, though, don't you think?''

''You'll be living with the results for the rest of your life,'' he said impatiently. ''What if the guy just neglected to mention that diabetes runs rampant in his family? Or schizophrenia? Or that he's got other hereditary diseases or conditions in his genetic makeup that could affect your child?''

''They screen the donations for genetic problems and diseases,'' she said. ''All the donors have complete physicals and genetic work-ups. I have some literature on it.''

''But they couldn't possibly check for everything,'' he pointed out. ''And are there background checks to see if these men are telling the truth about themselves?''

''I...I don't know. I doubt it.'' Jessie looked shell-shocked. ''But they're supposed to fill in everything they know.''

''And maybe they do.'' He made a deliberate effort to soften his censorious tone. ''Probably 99 percent of these men are honest and trustworthy. Hell, maybe they all are. But you have to assume that there could be some false-hoods, for your own protection.''

Jessie sighed deeply. ''Darn it, Ryan. I should have known I'd be more confused than I already am after I'd talked with you.''

''Thank you,'' he said.

''It *wasn't* a compliment.'' But she smiled. Reaching across the table, she took the folder from him and replaced it in her satchel, then shook her head. Her eyes were troubled. ''I was planning to do this the next time I ovulate, but I can see this is going to require a lot more thought than I'd anticipated.''

He couldn't dredge up an appropriate response to that, so he merely murmured, "Good."

The rest of the meal went quickly. She declined coffee, telling him she had to get back to relieve one of her sales staff, and they parted outside the Ritz. As he bent to kiss her cheek and she tilted her face up to his, the sweet scent of her filled him with an unexpectedly sharp longing, and he nearly closed his arms about her before he could catch himself. Unaware of his mental turmoil, Jessie backed away a step and waggled her fingers at him with an impish grin. "Same time, same place next month, big boy."

He managed a wave and stood for a long moment as she turned and walked down Arlington Street. Finally he turned and moved off in the other direction, taking a right on Beacon Street past the Public Garden and the Commons, heading back to his office on State Street in the financial district.

As he paced off the steps, his mind churned. What had happened back there? It was just that he missed having a woman in his life, he assured himself. Since his wife's death in a traffic accident, he'd led a lonely life. Being half of a couple had suited him. It had felt comfortable. He hated going home to the costly mansion in Brookline now, hated the silence after the day staff had left in the evening. He hated attending cocktail parties and charity events and having eager mothers thrusting their oh-so-eligible daughters in his path. The bottom line was that he simply hated being single.

And then there was the thought of children, which he'd put out of his mind years ago. Until Jessie's bright idea had dredged it up again.

Children. A stab of longing pierced him. He'd wanted

kids with Wendy, always assumed they'd start a family someday…but it hadn't been quite that simple. And now she was gone.

So marry Jessie. She wants a baby…you want a family.

The idea was so shocking that he stopped dead in the middle of the sidewalk on Tremont Street, causing a woman walking past to glance at him oddly.

Marry Jessie. The thought made his heart race alarmingly. Wryly, he acknowledged that some things never changed. Part of him was still that adolescent boy with the crush on his lissome young neighbor.

Marry Jessie. She was as different from his deceased wife as two women could be. Wendy had been blond and blue-eyed, petite and yet buxom. She'd been quietly charming, almost passive, rarely arguing with him. She'd been content to make a home for them; she'd felt no need to prove herself in a career. She'd been musical and elegant. Each night when he'd come home there'd been drinks in the drawing room.

Jessie…Jessie wasn't any of those things. Except elegant. With those long legs and the graceful way she carried herself, she was most definitely that. His mouth curved at the mere notion of Jess sitting home waiting for any man. She was volatile, determined to succeed at her business. If she disagreed with him, she said so in no uncertain terms. She had a tin ear, although she got offended if anyone suggested that perhaps she shouldn't sing.

For the first time, the striking differences made him pause. Could he have chosen Wendy, in part, *because* she was so completely unlike Jess?

It was an unnerving thought. He'd told himself he was over Jessie, that she'd been an adolescent fantasy. He'd married another woman and forgotten her. But in the back of his mind, he had to admit that it was possible he'd been comparing other women to her for the past ten years or more. And he *was* over her, he assured himself. Just because he couldn't stop thinking about her now didn't mean anything except that he was still as physically attracted to her as he'd always been.

So where did that leave him? Was it ridiculous to think that he could make a life with her now, a life that included the children he'd always wanted?

He'd reached his building, walking most of the way on automatic pilot while he'd thought of her, and as he stepped out of the elevator and walked down the hall to his office, a new determination hardened within him. The moment he'd hung up his coat and taken his messages from his office assistant, he went into his inner office and closed the door. Then he reached for the phone.

What did he have to lose?

After lunch Jessie was answering a customer's questions about a line of glazed pottery she carried when the telephone rang. Excusing herself, she moved to the phone. "The Reilly Gallery. May I help you?"

"Jess."

A small shock of surprise ran through her. "Ryan?" Normally she didn't see or hear from him from one month to the next unless they crossed paths at some social function. "Did I forget something?"

"No." There was an odd quality to his voice, as if he were unsure of something. "I wondered if...I'm calling to ask you to have dinner with me."

Dinner. With Ryan. "Why?"

He chuckled, and abruptly he sounded like the adult she'd come to know, self-confident and calm. "I had some

other thoughts about your, um, selection process that I
wanted to discuss with you.''

"Oh." Well, that was good, wasn't it? After what he'd
said at lunch, she'd been in a blue funk thinking about
the risks. "When and where?''

"How's tomorrow night? I'll pick you up. Seven all
right?''

"Tomorrow evening works for me. And seven is fine.''
What she really wanted to say was that tomorrow night
was *soon*. But she didn't have any reason to delay, and
she didn't even know why she instinctively wanted to do
so.

When she hung up the phone, her assistant had taken
over with the customer she'd been helping, so she headed
into her small office. On her desk was a loan application
she'd picked up from her bank on the way back to the
gallery after lunch. Ryan's question, "What are you going
to do about it?" had occupied her thoughts during the
walk, and she'd realized she had little choice. If she
wanted to compete, she was going to have to expand. And
to expand, she'd either have to get a loan, or use the
money she'd set aside for the artificial insemination. And
using that fund wasn't something she was prepared to do.

Thoughtfully she stared at the application. Although she
regularly paid on the loan she'd taken out when she
started her store, she had a line of credit that was running
a little higher than it should right now. It was a temporary
thing, based largely on the inventory she'd recently ordered in anticipation of the spring and summer tourist
season. But she suspected she'd have to pay it down before she could get a loan. And then there were the sales
figures…it would take a few days to pull all that together.

Another loan. Or, if she rolled her current one into it,
a larger loan. The mere thought made her nervous. She'd

worked hard to get to where she was now. She could pay
her bills, live comfortably and save for a leisurely retire-
ment someday. To her, loans meant that someone else
would own what she'd worked so hard to build, and with
that came the implied threat of loss. Her business was her
independence; she *couldn't* lose it. Still, she shouldn't
have any trouble meeting her financial obligations even if
they increased. It would simply mean cutting her personal
spending and watching her pennies at the gallery. But she
wasn't at all sure she was going to look like a good bet
to Mr. Brockhiser, the lender at Boston Savings with
whom she would be dealing.

The rest of the afternoon was insane, and it wasn't until
Jessie closed the door to her apartment that evening that
she thought about Ryan again. Thoughtfully she put away
her coat, boots, scarf and gloves. Her home was only four
blocks from her shop, and like many Bostonians, she pre-
ferred to hoof it as much as possible rather than fight the
notoriously clogged roadways.

She was afraid Ryan might be right about the sperm
donations. How *did* she know that what she saw on those
profiles was accurate? The screening process had sounded
so complete when she first read through it. But the bottom
line was that this was, at best, a game of chance.

When she'd first gone to discuss the procedure at the
fertility center, they'd asked her if she had a donor lined
up or if she planned to select one from a cryobank's stock.
She'd never even considered asking any of her friends to
donate *sperm,* for heaven's sake! She'd thought it would
be far too embarrassing. Not to mention the fact that
something within her warned her against using a friend
for such a purpose. What if the guy wanted rights to her
child at some later date? Probably an irrational fear, but…
And what about the fact that most of the decent men she

knew were already married, some with children of their own? She couldn't, and shouldn't, generalize, but she knew it would bother *her* if an acquaintance asked the man she loved to donate sperm for another woman's child. Oh, she'd read about people who'd done it, but it just wasn't an approach she felt comfortable using.

So that left bachelors. Jessie shuddered. Most of the single men she knew were single for a reason. She'd dated a number of them and hadn't been impressed by one yet. How could she possibly ask a guy she didn't even like? Okay, so that meant she could really narrow down the list, she thought as she pulled a bag of premixed tossed salad from her refrigerator and poured some into a bowl. There was a chicken breast left over from the ones she'd baked last night for herself and her assistant manager, Penny, and as she carried the food and a glass of Napa Valley Zinfandel to the small table in her kitchen alcove, she grabbed a pen and paper to start a list.

Let's see. She swirled the wine and inhaled, appreciating the fruity odors before she took a first, experimental drink. There was Edmund Lloyd. He wasn't so bad, except for that little stutter he sometimes couldn't get past. Was that a hereditary trait? She put a little question mark by Edmund's name. She'd have to see what she could find out about stuttering on the Internet.

She thought some more. What about Charles Bakler? He was a dear. But...not the brightest crayon in the box. And she wanted her baby to be intelligent. She put a frowning face beside Charles's name.

Okay. Surely she could come up with more desirable single men that that! What about Ryan? *No.* She dismissed the idea almost as quickly as it popped into her head. She could never ask Ryan. Not an option. But still...to be fair, she should list him. So she did. She didn't write anything at all beside his name.

Geoff Vertler. A possibility, except he was a pretty hearty partier, and she wouldn't want to inadvertently give her baby a predisposition to alcoholism.

Laying down the pencil, Jessie exhaled a frustrated sigh. This was stupid! She didn't even know as much about these men as she did about the candidates she'd chosen from the sperm bank. *If* what they'd written was true.

You know almost everything about Ryan, said that sneaky little voice in her head. Oh, Lord. She took a big slug of her wine. He really would be the logical choice. The one man she'd known nearly her entire life. He was smart, he was kind, he didn't have any horrible health secrets hidden in his family history. He was well coordinated, she knew, since he'd played soccer in high school and college, and he could even sing. Physically, he was…perfect. If she had a son who looked exactly like Ryan, she'd be thrilled.

But how could she ask him? Shaking her head, she pushed away from the table and rose. No way. She just couldn't.

But as she rinsed her dishes and put them in the dishwasher, a thought struck her. She was having dinner with him tomorrow night. And he'd said he had some other ideas to share with her. What if he was planning to offer to be the donor for her baby? She put a hand to her mouth—that had to be it! Why else would he want to have dinner? They normally had their monthly luncheon and went their separate ways.

Jessie danced down the hallway to her bedroom. It was perfect! She'd never have been able to approach him about it, but if he offered…just perfect. And she didn't have to worry about offending his wife since he didn't have one.

The thought doused her good humor, and she slowly tugged off her clothes and donned the oversize T-shirt in which she slept. It was purely an accident that Ryan didn't have a wife anymore. An awful, unexpected accident.

Climbing into bed, she set her alarm and snapped off the bedside lamp. But sleep eluded her.

She'd been at the University of Alabama getting her degree when Ryan had met Wendy, and she hadn't come home for the wedding. And by the time she'd come back to Boston, they had married, and Ryan already had begun to make history and money with the invention that had founded his fortune.

Wendy. She could still remember the ridiculous stab of jealousy she'd felt the first time Ryan had introduced them. Wendy had been petite and curvy, with big, arresting blue eyes and pretty cornsilk hair. She'd clung shyly to Ryan's hand, and Jessie had been jolted by the fierce feeling of possessiveness that had shot through her. Ryan had been *her* friend; for years and years the first person to whom she ran when things went wrong was the boy next door. Two years older, quiet and intelligent, he'd helped her survive what she now realized was an emotionally abusive childhood. They'd had a special bond. And though it had dimmed when she'd begun going steady with the captain of the high school football team and nearly died when she'd followed Chip south to Alabama, Ryan still had been *hers* in some indefinable way.

Jessie had chided herself for being childish and resolved to be pleasant to Wendy Shaughnessy, and to her surprise it hadn't been a chore. If there was a sweeter person alive, someone would have to prove it to Jessie.

Wendy had become a dear friend. In fact, it was she who had suggested the monthly luncheon tradition.

Who would have thought they'd be carrying on without her after only six short years?

And who, she asked herself wryly just before she finally fell asleep, ever would have imagined that Ryan would father Jessie's child? But she was sure that's what he was going to suggest. She could hardly wait for tomorrow evening!

Two

He took her to L'Espalier, a converted town house that had become one of Back Bay's premiere restaurants. It was only a few blocks from her home, but Jessie had never been there before. Partly because it was quite pricey, but also because L'Espalier was one of those places people went to celebrate life's milestones.

Over a truly superb vegetarian meal, though, Ryan showed no signs of getting around to the reason he'd asked her there. Much as they had yesterday, he kept the conversation impersonal, telling her about various causes for which he'd recently been solicited, asking her opinion on which ones would be the best to support. Maybe he'd changed his mind. Her heart sank. Could she force herself to ask him?

When she declined dessert, he asked for the check, and before she knew it, they were back on Marlborough Street, heading for her apartment. They both were silent as they walked along the sidewalk. Each of them had their gloved hands in their pockets, and walked carefully through the darkened streets; there were icy patches in unexpected places left over from a storm the week before.

Twice she opened her mouth and closed it without speaking. How to bring up the topic? Maybe he felt as embarrassed as she did. Maybe she should just go ahead and ask him. But she couldn't. Her vocal cords simply froze at the thought of asking Ryan to donate sperm. At the same time she was all too aware of his tall, broad-shouldered figure. She'd never looked at him as anything but a dear friend in the most platonic sense, but the whole notion of creating a child raised the specter of sexual intimacy, and try as she might, she couldn't rid herself of a new fascination with him. She would not, she reminded herself for at least the fiftieth time, engage in prurient thoughts about this man who'd been such a dear friend.

Right.

He had grown into an extraordinarily attractive man. His dark hair was thick and glossy and his eyes were a striking blue, made even more vivid when he had a tan through the summer months. As a child and a teenager he'd been tall but scrawny and awkward. Once he'd begun weight training, his arms had become muscular and strong. Apparently, he'd kept up some sort of fitness routine, because his shoulders now were almost bulky, and his upper arms filled out the sleeves of his suit jackets.

Stop it! Jessie told herself. Again. Ryan was her friend, not a potential lover. She ignored the quickening of her pulse.

In a few more moments they were back at her apartment building. In the hallway outside her door, she turned to him. But before she could speak, he said, "May I come in? I asked you out tonight for a purpose and I've been trying to get around to it all evening." He smiled wryly. "Trying to work up my courage."

Relief washed through her. "Of course. I've been wondering about it. How about if I make us some coffee?"

"Sounds good." He followed her as she unlocked her door and stepped into the small foyer.

Jessie took his coat and waved him into the living room while she hung up their outerwear and went into the kitchen to start some coffee. She put a paper doily on a small plate, then got some grapes from the bowl on her counter and arranged them on the tray with a handful of peanut butter cookies she'd gotten from the deli down the street on her way home earlier. Pulling out a tray, she set the plate on it along with creamer, sugar and spoons. She was pretty sure he drank his coffee black.

In another moment her little coffeemaker had finished, and she poured two cups. Walking into the living room, she set the tray on the table before the sofa and took a seat. Ryan had been standing at the window, looking out into the dark night. But when he heard her, he turned and came over to stand near her. "Sit down," she invited, patting the cushion beside her.

"Thanks." He did so, then picked up his cup and took a drink, grimacing at the heat. She noted with satisfaction that she'd been right—he drank it black. "Your apartment's nice," he said. "I've never seen where you live before."

"I don't do the hostess thing," she said. "It's too small for parties. But given the price of real estate in Back Bay right now, I'm lucky to have it at all."

There was a small, awkward silence between them.

Finally, Ryan stirred and turned toward her. "Jessie, we've been friends for a long time. I know you want children.'' He took a deep breath. ''And so do I. Will you marry me?''

What? She couldn't have heard him right. But she knew she had, and her voice showed her agitation when she spoke. ''No! Ryan, that's not what I want—I mean, you don't really want to marry me, either. When you called, I thought…I thought…''

''You thought what?'' His voice was flat and distant as he stared into his coffee cup.

She felt a blush creeping up her neck into her cheeks. ''Well, I thought you were going to offer to be a…a donor.''

''You what?'' His mouth dropped open much as hers had a moment before, and his gaze shot to hers.

''I thought about what you said all day.'' She rushed on, wanting only to get this over with. ''You're right about anonymous men being risky. So I decided it would be better to ask someone I know to be a donor. But most of my friends are married, and I didn't really feel comfortable…so I made a list of bachelors—''

''And my name was at the top of your list?'' His voice sounded incredulous and his distaste was clear.

''Well, yes.'' She looked away from the cool blue eyes. ''I've known you practically forever and I know your family.'' She shrugged. ''It seemed like a logical idea.'' She could see from the dark frown that drew his brows into a single thick line that he was about to refuse so she kept on. ''Please, Ry? I'm serious about this baby. It would really, really mean a lot to me.''

But he shook his head. ''I don't think so, Jess.''

''But why?'' She was pleading and she knew it.

''I wouldn't be—I'm not comfortable with the idea that a child of mine would be raised never knowing me, never knowing I'm its father.'' He shook his head again, decisively, and her heart sank. "It would bother me not to be involved in my child's life."

"This is exactly the reaction I was afraid most of my married friends would have." She made an effort to soften her tone. "But I didn't expect it from you."

"I didn't expect it from me, either, but then I never expected *you* to ask me to do something like this." He looked down into his coffee cup again, hesitated, then shook his head. "I couldn't do it, Jess. It wouldn't be my child, legally, but I'd feel connected, responsible. I'd want to hold it, to play with it, to watch it grow up and be involved in its life. I can't imagine knowing I had a child somewhere in the world and not being a father to it." He spread his hands. "I want kids of my own. I want to give a child memories as wonderful as the ones I have of my own parents."

She was stunned by the passion in his voice. Her throat felt thick as she remembered the two people who had raised Ryan and his brother, the two people who had opened their arms and their hearts and included her in their charmed circle anytime she entered their home.

She cleared her throat. "I never even knew you wanted children." She spread her hands. "You were married to Wendy for six years—"

"Wendy couldn't conceive." His voice was harsh now and abrupt. He stood so suddenly he knocked against the table, and the coffee sloshed in the cups. Stalking over to the window, he shoved his jacket back and put his hands on his hips. "We wanted them. Badly. But we tried for three years with no luck and then spent another one finding out what the problem was. We tried in-vitro fertilization twice but no luck. And then she died."

She eyed the rigid line of his shoulders, and her heart squeezed painfully. She'd been thinking selfishly and was sick at heart that she'd inadvertently caused him sadness. Softly she said, "I'm sorry to bring up something painful to you. If I'd known, I never would have—"

"It's not exactly something you want to share with the world." His voice was curt.

Hurt pierced her heart. She wasn't "the world." She'd thought she was his oldest friend. But apparently, in his mind, that old bond didn't mean the same thing it still meant to her. She felt the hot sting of tears at the backs of her eyes and she strove to breathe deeply, to stay calm.

At the window Ryan turned, and she quickly dropped her head. As she did so, one fat tear plopped down onto her hands, tightly clenched in her lap. Smoothing it away with her thumb, she kept her head bent as he resumed his seat beside her.

"Jess?" His voice was quiet. "I don't want to argue with you. You mean too much to me."

"You mean a lot to me, too," she said. And then her voice broke and she turned at the same instant he did, moving into the arms he held wide.

Jessie had danced with Ryan before, hugged him occasionally, brushed quick friendly kisses on his cheek. But she'd never known she'd find such comfort in his embrace. Even when his parents had died, they hadn't shared a closeness like this. He'd had Wendy to comfort him then. Now his arms were hard and muscled beneath the fabric of his jacket, his shoulder a wide plane just right for her head. When she felt him press a kiss into her hair, she smiled. "I have a great idea," she said.

"What's that?" His voice rumbled up from beneath her ear.

"Let's forget this whole stupid conversation. Just pretend it never existed."

He was quiet for a moment. "If that's what you want."

She frowned, drawing back and looking him in the eye. "Isn't that what you want?"

He shrugged, hesitated. Finally he said, "I still think marriage would be a good plan, if you want to know the truth. We both want the same thing, Jess. I think we could be happy together."

She sighed. "We're never going to go back to the way we were, are we?" she asked sadly.

Soberly he shook his head. "Doubt it."

Fear shot through her at the cool, measured tone. The last thing she wanted was to lose him altogether. Reluctantly she said, "All right." She folded her hands in her lap. "Explain exactly why you think we should get married." *Get married...get married...* The words echoed in her head. Was she really having *this* conversation with *this* man?

"Okay." He stood and began to walk the length of her living room, such as it was. "Selfish reasons first. Number one—I've got ridiculous numbers of women throwing themselves at me ever since that stupid article came out. You saw how it is today. Marriage would kill all that."

"One of them might make a good wife." But she hoped not.

He shook his head. "Any woman who would come on to a man like that is *not* a woman I'd want to date, much less marry."

"Maybe not." She shouldn't feel so relieved by his terse words. After all, she didn't want to marry him. Did she? Of course not. Ryan deserved to find another woman like Wendy, a woman who would adore him and whom he could adore in return. It wouldn't be fair at all to trap him into marriage to her simply because they shared a history and a common goal.

You both could do a lot worse, pointed out a small devil's voice inside her head.

That might be true, but what if it didn't work out? A tremor ran through her at the mere idea. She didn't think she could bear losing Ryan, as she surely would if they married and it was a disaster. He'd been the rock that anchored her stormy childhood, and he still was her dearest friend in all the world. She couldn't—*wouldn't*—do anything to jeopardize that.

"Number two." Unaware of her mental deliberations, he held up two fingers of his right hand. "I liked being married. I liked coming home to someone, sharing meals, sharing conversation. Wendy and I were friends. We could talk about anything." He looked at her. "You and I have that, too."

Jessie nodded. But she was very aware that there was one thing he hadn't mentioned sharing in a marriage: a bed. A tingle of awareness shot through her, shocking her with its intensity.

"Number three," he went on. "I want children. Of my own. Running through my house making noise, breaking windows with baseballs—"

"They might be girls," she said automatically, still preoccupied by the strange feelings rioting through her.

But Ryan didn't respond. He stopped pacing, his back to her, and she could see the tension in the rigid set of his shoulders and the way his head drooped. Sensing pain in his silence, she rose and went to him, wrapping her arms around him from behind as far as they would go.

The butterflies that had been plaguing her returned the moment she touched him. He felt bulky and muscular, warm beneath her hands, and his strong back, against which she pressed herself, was as unyielding as steel. He smelled of some expensive cologne and the clean scent of drycleaned wool. Then he turned, dislodging her hold. Placing his hands on her shoulders, he bent his head and kissed her temple.

Her breath caught in her throat and she stepped back, giving him room. As she lifted her gaze to face him, he said, "So what are your objections?"

She shook her head. "When you get hold of an idea, you don't let go, do you?"

He grinned. "Just noticing?"

She smiled, then crossed her arms and lifted a finger to tap her lips. "Objections. Hmm." She spread her hands, loath to put all the things running through her head into words. "I don't know. I haven't even given marriage a thought since I was too young to know better."

"With what's-his-name."

"His name was Chip and you know it. You never liked him, did you?"

Ryan shrugged. "Maybe I just didn't think he was good enough for you."

She laughed. "You were right. And thank God I figured it out before I married him!" Then she sobered. "Actually, he was a great guy. Just not for me. I realized that I liked the things I got from him—security, adoration, the illusion of belonging—a lot more than I liked *him*. And marriage wouldn't have been fair to him." She fell silent.

"Back to your objections," he prompted.

"I don't *know*," she protested. "I suppose I always assumed that when I married it would be for the usual reasons."

"The usual reasons?"

"You know. Love," she said, throwing her arms wide. "And passion."

As soon as the words were out, she saw his face change. Though he hadn't moved, she suddenly felt as if all the air in the room were supercharged. A strange, wild flame leaped, deep in his blue eyes, and his gaze dropped to her mouth, igniting a quivering spark in her abdomen that made her catch her breath in shock. "Passion, I can promise you," he said, his voice soft and low.

Jessie was stunned. This was *Ryan,* for heaven's sake! Her friend.

But the feelings coursing through her weren't those of friendship. She felt as though an invisible cord inexorably tugged her toward him. She could almost feel his strong arms around her again. Her body ached to feel him pressed against her, and her lips practically tingled beneath his intent gaze.

Good Lord. How had she not noticed how incredibly sexy he was for all these years? Or had she? Had she simply refused to acknowledge the deep pull of attraction between them? After all, he'd been married.

"Ryan?" Her voice sounded like a stranger's.

He took a step toward her, and she instinctively put out a hand to hold him off. But he took it and tugged her toward him. "Don't you think we should explore what we could have between us?" Pulling her into his arms, he folded her firmly against him. Her hands splayed wide over his biceps. She intended to push him away, but her limbs felt weak and shaky, and when he didn't release her, she simply stood in his embrace, feeling the erotic electricity that flowed from him to her. She was shockingly aware of his hard body against hers, of the checked power in his close hold.

Jessie's teeth were practically chattering with nerves. "I…I don't know. I never thought about you—about me and you—as anything more than friends." She felt tears fill her eyes yet again. "You're the best friend I have in the whole world, and I don't want to screw things up and lose you. I *need* you to be my friend, Ry.''

Silence fell. Ryan didn't move. He didn't release her, nor did he tighten his arms. She kept her head down, knowing that if she raised her face to his right now this whole discussion would be moot, and their relationship would change forever. And despite the words of caution she'd just uttered, she couldn't stop herself from wondering what it would be like with Ryan. Would he be slow and gentle or as hot and wild as the sensations ripping through her right now? She saw again in her mind the light in his eyes and heard his deep, rough voice: *Passion I can promise you.*

His hands were on her back, and as he shifted them slightly, rubbing gentle patterns over her sensitive flesh, she shuddered. Had she ever wanted to cast rational thought to the winds so badly? Her body warred with her mind for another long moment. But finally she heaved a deep sigh and pushed back from his embrace. This time he let her go.

''No,'' she said, trying to invest her tone with a firmness she didn't feel. ''This wouldn't be right.'' She turned away, hugging her arms tightly about herself. ''I'm sorry.'' She knew the words were inadequate, but her throat felt as if someone were squeezing it with a vise.

Behind her she heard his footsteps as he went to the closet and took out his coat. Fabric rustled as he donned his outerwear, then he walked to her, stepping into her line of vision and lifting her chin with one finger. Jessie had been standing with her eyes closed, but she forced herself to open them and gaze into his blue ones.

And the moment she did, she knew that nothing would be as it had been before. Awareness leaped and crackled between them like well-fed flames.

"All right," he said. "Friends it is. But the offer of marriage still stands. Think about it."

She nodded, unable to trust her voice.

He dropped his hand from her face, stepped away. "Good night."

Jessie didn't sleep well that night. Or any night for the rest of the week. On Saturday she threw away the preliminary profiles of the donors. Although she didn't believe the process carried the risks that Ryan thought it did, it seemed impersonal and distasteful to her now.

On Sunday she walked through the Public Gardens. A young couple passed her, their faces alive with laughter as their toddler, awkward and stiff in layers of bulky winter clothing, ran in circles until she was dizzy. As the father scooped the pink-cheeked child into his arms, the baby squealed with laughter, and Jessie felt her heart contract with pain.

Why shouldn't she have that joy? Just because she hadn't been lucky enough to find someone with whom she could share her life—

Ah, but you had someone, her inner self reminded her. *And you gave him away.*

Chip. She'd been courted by a star member of the football team during her first year of high school. At the time, she hadn't given the guy behind the persona a serious thought. He'd been popular; every girl in the school had envied her. At fifteen, that was what it all had been about. In her naïveté, she'd never really thought about the fact that they had next to nothing in common. To her he'd represented safety. Security. Someone who loved her unconditionally, darn near worshipped her, for heaven's sake. In her whole life there had never been anyone like that. Ryan had been her lifeline during her childhood, but he'd distanced himself when she began dating Chip, and she'd rarely seen him after he'd left for college. Looking back, she almost felt as if he'd abandoned her. Was it any wonder she had followed Chip south to school?

It wasn't until she'd gotten to college that she'd begun to grow and change, to realize that the world was a big place and her choices were limitless. And as she had, she'd realized that she could never make a life with Chip.

She'd been fond of him, but she hadn't loved him. To marry him would have been unfair to them both. She'd used him as a crutch for a very long time, and she prayed that he'd found some sweet girl and was married, that they were happily raising half a dozen little football players and cheerleaders.

And that thought brought her back to her present problem. She could have married and had children with Chip. But…something had stopped her. She hadn't known at the time exactly why he wasn't right. She'd just known he wasn't.

And after she'd settled down in Boston and gotten her shop established, she hadn't found the right man, either.

Will you marry me?

Ryan's words echoed over and over again in her head. Was it possible she'd been tempted to blurt out, "Yes!" for one ridiculous, impetuous instant?

Familiarity, she decided. Ryan had known her forever. He knew all her warts and quirks. They had a number of interests in common. Living with Ryan would be comfortable in many ways.

But as she remembered the breathless, shocking awareness that had swamped her when he'd taken her in his arms, the word *comfortable* wasn't the one that seemed to apply.

That line of thought was dangerous. Her mind shied

away from any examination of exactly what had happened last night. Instead she focused on his refusal to help her in her quest for motherhood. She should have realized, would have, if she'd thought about it longer, that Ryan Shaughnessy would have difficulty with the concept of a biological child to which he had no rights or attachment.

Ryan's family had been a close and loving one. She should know. Hadn't she sought refuge in Mrs. Shaughnessy's plump arms more than once? Mr. Shaughnessy had been warm and boisterous, including her in the games of pitch-and-catch with Ryan and his older brother, tossing her high in the air just to hear her scream. And on the occasions when she'd eaten at the Shaughnessy house, the teasing camaraderie and open love in their home had never failed to amaze her.

Her family had been very different. Her mother, as far as Jessie could tell, felt that raising a child was little more than a duty. Her grandparents regarded her as a trial, a punishment sent by God for some unfathomable crime. They had failed as parents when their only daughter had gotten herself pregnant and, even worse, refused to marry—or even name—the father of her baby.

Unless they'd been a lot different during her mother's childhood, Jessie thought it likely that her mother had succumbed to the first man ever to say a kind word to her. A mistake Jessie herself very nearly had made with Chip, although he'd been quite different from the man who'd apparently seduced and waltzed away from her mother.

No, thank goodness she'd gotten smart. She wasn't *ever* going to believe that a man was her ticket to fulfillment. She knew better.

And where did that leave her? Alone, childless, aching for her life to mean something to somebody. Which was why, if she was honest with herself, she felt so strongly about having a child of her own.

She thought again of her fears, weighed them against the certainty of years passing her by. Could she marry Ryan? Perhaps he was right about their friendship being a good basis for the marriage. But…what if she didn't conceive? What would happen then? She had friends who had infertility problems, and the uncertainties put a strain on even the most devoted couple. What would happen to a couple like Ryan and her if something like that happened?

And then it struck her. What if they compromised? What if she agreed to marry Ryan if, and only if, he gave her a baby? She hadn't thought that her baby needed a father. After all, she'd survived without one. What her baby needed was love, and that she knew she could give it. But she also knew Ryan. He'd said marriage, and she knew he'd never go for anything less.

And the thought of giving her child a warm, loving, *complete* family was very seductive. Maybe they could even have more than one child. Then it struck her—additional children would be conceived far more conventionally if this all came to pass. She'd be tacitly agreeing to a lasting sexual arrangement with Ryan. And in good conscience, she couldn't pretend that would be a problem.

The real problem might be keeping her hands *off* him.

She shivered suddenly, though she was walking down Marlborough Street now at a brisk pace. Her mind racing, she considered the idea from all angles. As she reached the steps of her building, she nodded once, sharply, then went inside and headed straight for the phone.

When Ryan's deep voice said, "Hello?" though, for a moment her throat seized up, and she couldn't speak.

"Jessie? Is that you?" His voice was sharp enough to startle her into speech again.

"How did you know?" she asked.

"Caller I.D."

"Oh."

Silence.

"Jess? Did you call me for a reason or did you just want to breathe heavily into the phone?"

"I want to talk to you again. About this baby stuff."

On the other end of the phone, he sighed. "I don't believe there's any point in talking it to death."

"I had an idea," she said. "Could you meet me for dinner?"

"Three meals in two days. All my adoring fans are going to start to worry."

"Maybe they should."

"Jess—"

"Come on, Ryan. Live dangerously. The East Coast Grill? Seven o'clock?"

"Wow. All the way over in Cambridge? I didn't know you strayed that far from home."

"Very funny. Will you do it?"

"All right," he said. "But only because I know you'll bug me to death until I listen to you. I'm telling you right up front that there is no way I am going to change my mind."

"I understand," she said. "All I ask is that you listen."

When she arrived in a taxi at 7:05 he already was waiting. To her eternal amusement he was seated at the bar with a woman on each side of him apparently vying for his attention.

Jessie walked up behind them and put her hands over his eyes. "Guess who?"

"Hey, there." He swiveled around on his stool to face her. "You're early."

The women who'd been speaking to him were eyeing her with something less than friendliness. An imp of mischief seized her, and she placed her hands on either side of Ryan's face, leaning forward and giving him a quick peck on the lips. "Miss me?"

"Always." She hadn't counted on his quick reflexes. His hands came up before she could draw away. One shackled her wrist, the other cradled the back of her head as he returned a second, much more leisurely kiss. His lips were warm and firm, molding her own as her heart thudded, and she nearly sank into the promise inherent in the lingering caress before she remembered who she was kissing and why. When he let her go, she drew back, flustered.

He rose and settled a hand at her waist, turning to smile at the women as Jessie blinked and forced herself to focus. "It was nice meeting you."

As he seated her and moved around the small table, she sent him an easy grin, determined not to let him see she'd been shaken by that kiss. "Was I helpful?"

"Infinitely." He shrugged out of his leather jacket. "I was being accosted."

"Well," she said, "it's not every day a girl gets to meet an eminently available hunk."

"If I hear that phrase out of you one more time," he said, leaning forward with mock menace, "your derriere is going to meet my eminently available hand."

She smiled brilliantly. "Ooooh, sounds like fun. Promise?"

His eyes narrowed, and that quickly the playful moment metamorphosed into something entirely different, something dark and dangerous with undercurrents of an intensity that caught her breath in her throat.

"Okay. You folks want to order drinks?" The arrival of the server broke through the stillness between them.

She sat quietly as Ryan ordered their drinks. What was happening to her? And to the comfortable, familiar relationship she'd had with Ryan?

"So," he said when the waitress had returned with their drinks and taken their dinner orders, "what new wrinkle in your mind was so urgent that you had to see me again tonight?"

"I was thinking about what you said." She spoke slowly, cautiously.

"I've said a lot of things to you," he said, unhelpful. "Want to be a tad more specific?"

"About marriage." The words fell between them, their ripples widening, breaking up the smooth surface of the conversation.

His eyes grew more intense, bluer; she felt like a mouse caught in the cat's corner. "What about it?"

"Well, I was thinking." She stopped, swallowed. "If you were to donate—and I did get pregnant—we could maybe get married once the baby was born. I mean, it would be stupid of us to marry assuming we were going to be parents. A lot of things can happen during pregnancy and I wouldn't want to trap you into anything if it didn't—"

"Stop." He held up a hand, palm out. "You're babbling."

"Sorry. I'm nervous." She fell silent, biting her lip. "I just thought—"

His eyebrows rose. "You've been doing quite a lot of thinking lately." He picked up his wineglass and gently swirled the Merlot they were drinking, tilting the glass and absently studying the color of the wine. "Let me see if I understand what you're proposing. I donate sperm. You, hopefully, get pregnant. If the pregnancy goes to term and we have a child, we marry."

She nodded, too embarrassed to look him in the eye but relieved that he'd grasped the idea. "Exactly."

"No." He sat back in his chair, crossing one long leg over the other.

"No?" Startled, she leaned forward and glared at him. "Why not? I thought you would be happy. This way we both get what we want."

"It makes me uncomfortable," he said. "Where's the guarantee that you'll keep your end of the bargain once you get what you want?"

She was stung by the implication that he didn't trust her. "That's not a very nice thing to say. Have I ever given you reason to distrust my word?"

He shrugged. "No. But this is a life-changing discussion we're having here, not a promise to water my plants while I'm out of town."

She had to admit he had a point. But she was still annoyed. "So call a lawyer if I'm so sneaky. I'll sign a contract."

Ryan was silent. His eyes regarded her intently until she was the first to look away. Finally he sighed. "Okay, here's another compromise. You get pregnant. If everything goes all right for the first couple of months…"

"The first trimester," she said, showing off her knowledge.

"Right. If everything goes well through the first trimester, we marry then. I don't want my child born out of wedlock."

She sighed. "You are an amazingly old-fashioned fuddy-duddy."

His broad shoulders rose and fell again. "An eminently available fuddy-duddy, though. There are lots of women who would leap at the chance to marry me and have my babies."

It would have been the perfect opportunity to say, *Fine. Let one of them have you.* But her tongue wouldn't wrap itself around the words. Something inside her recoiled from the idea of another woman bearing his children. And hadn't she decided he'd be a perfect biological father for her own? A perfect father in many ways? A perfect husband— She cut off that thought before it took root.

"It's not just being old-fashioned," he said suddenly. "I'm helping you out. You can return the favor. If I'm married, there won't be any more of those annoying articles."

He had a point. And the reminder that this would be something of an exchange of favors made her feel better. It was nice that she wasn't the only one getting something out of the arrangement. "All right." She spoke slowly, cautiously. "I guess we could get married if the early part of the pregnancy goes well."

He nodded once. "It's a deal, then."

The waiter returned with their dinners. Ryan had the barbecue that had been one of the Grill's outstanding specialties for years. She'd ordered the Grilled Sausage from Hell. Though it was wonderful, she could only manage to eat about half of it, so Ryan polished off the rest as well as his own meal.

"So what happens next?" he asked as their plates were removed.

"I'm monitoring my cycle. I'll use an ovulation kit to determine when we go. I'm pretty regular so it'll probably be the middle of next week."

"Stop." He held up a hand. "I know the rest. We

talked about artificial insemination when Wendy and I were going through this, but ultimately we learned her fallopian tubes were blocked.''

She nodded. The same sense of shock and hurt that she'd felt when he'd first told her about Wendy's and his infertility treatments rolled through her again. ''I cannot believe you never told me about that.''

He looked away. ''Like I said, it was a very personal thing.''

And none of her business. She read between the lines. ''I'm sorry,'' she said. ''I don't mean to be nosy.'' She hesitated. ''I guess it bothers me a little that there are these big parts of your life about which I know nothing. We shared just about everything growing up, didn't we?''

''Not by a long shot.'' His answer was quick and sharp. ''After you started dating Mr. Football Star, there was a whole lot we didn't share.''

She was stunned by the vehemence in his tone. The Ryan she recalled from high school had been absorbed in academics and weight lifting. He'd rarely sought her out and often had little to say when she'd made time for him. Was it possible she'd hurt him somehow? Offended him without realizing it? She wanted to ask him, but she wasn't sure either of them was ready to open such a can of worms. ''Maybe we should just agree to start from this moment,'' she said carefully. ''If this works out, we could be sharing a family in less than a year.''

He nodded without looking at her. But after a moment he reached across the table and took her hand. ''Good idea,'' he said quietly. His palm engulfed hers and his thumb rubbed across the back of her knuckles gently, creating a warmth that sizzled up her arm into her bloodstream. A heavy pool of heat settled low in her abdomen and she shifted slightly in her seat. ''I have a good feeling about this," he told her. "We're going to be good together…in lots of ways."

The heat in her belly expanded, and her breathing grew short as her imagination shot vivid mental pictures of one way they could be good together across her mental screen. "I, ah, you're probably right." Hastily she pulled her hand from his. "Well, I have to work tomorrow so we'd better call it a night."

But as they parted outside the Grill, the impact of exactly how much her life was going to change as a result of this night hit her squarely in the face. She turned to Ryan, holding out both hands. "Thank you."

He smiled, his dimples carving deep grooves in his cheeks as he took her hands and squeezed them lightly. "Thank *you,* Jess. I'll call you tomorrow."

"All right." And as she hopped into her compact car for the short drive home, she found that she was practically jittering with excitement and happiness. But if she was honest with herself, it wasn't entirely the prospect of finally realizing her desire to have a baby that was at the heart of it.

She was going to marry Ryan if things went well. And though she never would have suspected it, she found the idea held immense appeal.

Three

She called him the following morning to tell him that the fertility center had confirmed that next week would be the best time for her to conceive if he wanted to "do it" right away. As he punched the off button on his office speaker phone, he knew a moment's relief that she still wanted to go through with the plan. He'd been afraid she would change her mind and go for an anonymous donor.

Ryan could have told her what he really wanted to do right away, but he had the feeling that might just send Jessie running for the hills. He wondered what was going through her mind at the thought of marriage to him. Had it even struck her yet that this would be permanent, a real marriage in every way? They hadn't talked at all about where they would live. About how many children they wanted or about whether or not she wanted to continue working.

About sex.

He was pretty sure she'd never thought about sex, about lovemaking, in connection with him before. In high school he'd been merely her pal, the guy next door. She'd begun dating the football player when she was a freshman, and they'd seen less of each other from that time on. Not that she had noticed.

No, he'd been the only one to suffer. He'd left for college at the end of the following year, but he'd kept tabs on her during his infrequent visits home, each time hoping against hope that she was free. Looking back, he didn't know if he'd have had the nerve to ask her out even if she had been, but it had been a moot point. Two years later she'd graduated and promptly headed south to Alabama.

That was when he'd let reality seep in around the edges of his dreams of a life with Jessie. And with reality had come Wendy. If Wendy had lived, he'd have remained faithful. His feelings for Jessie never would have gone anywhere outside his own mind.

But Wendy was gone. And Jessie had come to him with a proposition most sane men would have laughed at. Not him. Not with her.

How did she feel about him? Was there any hope that she wanted him as much as he wanted her? His euphoria faded. For the first time he fully appreciated the situation he was in. For years Jessie had been out of reach, and he'd resigned himself to a life without her. Suddenly he was faced with the possibility of sharing the rest of his life with her. But still, sweet as that thought was, it wasn't enough. It was a frustrating feeling for a man who controlled a significant financial empire, a man who'd met most challenges with success in the past decade.

The memory of her appalled reaction when he first mentioned marriage still stung. And last night, she'd almost hyperventilated when he'd obliquely mentioned sex. There definitely had been times when he'd have sworn there was attraction between them—was it just his longing that made it so?

No, he was pretty sure she felt something for him. Tonight, when he'd been holding her hand, she'd looked dazed and distinctly…aroused, just as she had earlier when he'd kissed her and her mouth had softened and clung to his. He'd found himself cursing the public place and the table between them. And when he'd nearly kissed her in her apartment that night, she'd trembled in his arms, and he'd felt the battle she was fighting with herself. She'd wanted him then. She'd wanted to lift her face to his and let the attraction roaring between them take over…but she'd backed off. *This wouldn't be right.* Why not? What was she hiding from him? Or was she hiding from herself?

After lunch, working on impulse, he picked up the phone in his office again and dialed the number of her store. After two rings, her brisk, business-like voice said, "The Reilly Gallery. May I help you?"

"I'm beyond help," he said. Something within him seemed to calm and settle at the sound of her voice. He was, indeed, beyond help.

She laughed, and her voice softened. "Hi."

"Hi, yourself. Having a busy afternoon?"

"Not especially."

"Good. I wanted to ask you where you want to live."

She was silent for a long time. "Live?"

"Yeah. House, furniture, place to hang your hat. Home, dwelling, abode. Cottage, castle, condo—"

"Enough! I know what you meant. I guess I just figured…"

"Figured what?"

"Well, why don't we wait until we find out if there's going to be any need to get married before we start making plans?"

He wanted to tell her he had a need to marry her regardless of whether or not she got pregnant. But he could tell from the skittish tone of her voice that that probably wasn't the smartest thing he could say right now. So instead, he said, "Would you like to come to dinner on Saturday evening?"

"Come to dinner?" she echoed.

"At my home," he clarified. "I know you've been there a time or two, but this way you can look around the whole place and take your time thinking about what we should do about housing when and if we marry."

"I guess that's a good idea." Although she didn't sound sure.

"Great. I'll pick you up at seven."

"Oh, no. I can—"

"I'll pick you up," he repeated. "Seven on Saturday. See you then."

After he hung up, he swiveled his leather executive chair toward the window. His suite of offices was on the top floor of the towering building he'd purchased from one of the Russell heirs nine years ago. Looking out the window, he had a perfect view of the harbor and the bay beyond it, with boats of all shapes and sizes looking like toys around the wharves. To the north, Christopher Columbus Park along the waterfront was conspicuously pristine beneath its mantle of white snow as the Atlantic Avenue traffic flowed past it.

He was a wealthy man. The view before him proved it—his office was in the heart of Boston's financial district—and yet he still felt like the tongue-tied kid from the Irish enclave whenever he talked to Jessie. The next few months were going to be difficult, he sensed. It was his nature to push forward, to maneuver and outflank until he'd gotten what he was after. But if he continued to try to press Jessie, he was sure to fail.

Spinning his chair around again, he looked over his calendar. Before this…arrangement had come about with Jess, he'd been considering some travel to make his presence known at several of his other enterprises around the country. But now he thought he'd better reschedule. At least push his plans back until after they found out whether or not the artificial insemination worked.

She was ready when he arrived on Saturday evening and he drove her out to Brookline where his home was located. It was a straight drive out through the prestigious lower blocks of Commonwealth Avenue to the five-bedroom Georgian Revival mansion he and Wendy had purchased back when they still had dreams of filling it with a large family.

Although they parked in the garage behind the house, he had to drive around the block to get to it, and Jessie craned her neck as they passed the stately entrance on Commonwealth with its gracious bow front. It was easily the largest town home in the area.

"Did I ever tell you how much I admired your taste in a home?" she asked.

"No, but thank you." He hoped she liked it. He'd gotten sort of attached to the place. If she didn't, he'd buy something else that she liked better, though. He'd rather have Jessie than the house any day. *And a family,* he added silently, hastily. A family was the reason he wanted her so badly.

"Exactly how old is this house?"

"It was built in 1866." And he'd better stop thinking so much or he was going to be insane.

"Amazing."

She slanted him a smile as he helped her from the Mercedes and they walked through the winter gardens to the back entrance.

"This garden is nice in the spring and summer," he said. "I found a landscaper who does an outstanding job. He also takes care of the terrace on the roof."

"The terrace on the roof." She smiled. "Did you ever imagine, when you were a kid, that one day you'd own a Victorian mansion in the Back Bay?"

He shook his head. "My dreams ran more along the lines of getting the girl and finding a job. It's funny how this just...happened."

"It did not just happen. You made it happen."

He shrugged. "Maybe. But there was a certain amount of luck involved. I had the right idea at the right time and was lucky enough to get backing from a financier who had a weak moment." He showed her into the less formal family room, then held up a finger as he moved away. "Just let me find out what time Finn plans to serve the meal."

After a quick conference with the man who'd been with them since before Wendy's death, he reentered the family room.

Jessie was standing with her back to him at the bay windows that overlooked the back gardens. She turned and smiled when he came in, and the force of her smile smote him heavily in his vulnerable heart. "I know what you're doing," she said as he opened a bottle of Chenin Blanc and poured two glasses.

He raised an eyebrow as he crossed to her, handing her her drink. "You do?"

"You're trying to make me fall for your house so I'll agree to live here."

He swirled his wine and inhaled, enjoying the rich bouquet. "Is it working?"

"Probably. I had thought I'd like to stay close to the shop, but this really isn't that far and it's so lovely." She took an experimental sip of her own drink, then regarded him with concern in her eyes. "But..." She hesitated.

He waited.

"If it bothers you to stay here—I mean, you lived here with Wendy—"

"It's all right." He spoke quietly.

There was a short silence, then he spoke again. "Have you thought about whether or not you want to continue working after the baby's born?"

Her gaze flew to his, then bounced away. "I feel superstitious talking about this. You, of all people, know that it's not always easy to get pregnant."

"But I have a good feeling about it." And he did. Strangely, his experiences with Wendy didn't feature in his thoughts these days.

She looked at him, worrying her lower lip.

That small motion drove him crazy, for more reasons than one. "Stop that." He reached out and touched her bottom lip with his finger, gently tracing over the line of her lip just below where she had caught it between her teeth. "Your lips are too pretty to be damaged."

Instantly she released the lip. "Uh, thank you." Her voice was strangely husky.

"Here. I have something to show you." He turned away as if the intimate moment were nothing out of the ordinary. Jessie took a seat at his side as he settled himself on the couch.

"What is it?" she asked as he removed the lid of a large, square box.

"Photos." He reached into the tissue and extracted a worn black photo album. "I had a lot of Mom's and Dad's things put in storage, and recently I've been going through them. I found this last week. There are a few of you in here."

"Of me?" Her eyes grew big. "I can count on one hand the number of photos I have of myself other than school photos. Could I have copies made?"

He nodded. "Sure. Want to take a peek?"

She plopped herself down beside him, her arm brushing his. "Does a fish like water?"

Together they opened the old book. He hadn't gone through it all before. He hadn't had a surfeit of time, and if he were honest with himself, it was difficult. He'd had a good childhood, but his parents were gone now. His father had keeled over from a massive heart attack his last year in college, and his mother had died four years ago. His brother, Vinson, lived several hours away now, and those happy days when they'd run up and down the old streets of Charlestown with Jessie hot on their heels, shouting in her high treble voice, "Wait fo' me, guys!" were but a memory.

"Oh, look!" She pointed at a picture in the far corner. "There's the Big Brown Bomb."

The Bomb. He chuckled. He'd forgotten about the wood-paneled station wagon they'd once had. His father would pile a whole bunch of the neighborhood kids into it and take them for bouncing jaunts out into the Massachusetts countryside for the sheer pleasure of hearing the kids yell every time he gassed it over a bump in the road. "Remember the time Willy Evert threw up down the back of Dad's neck?"

She was holding her sides, laughing hard now. "I'll never forget it. Your dad nearly ran off the road trying to get out of his shirt."

Grinning fondly, they paged through the rest of the album, reminiscing over many of their shared antics. On the last page was a picture of the two of them on the day he started seventh grade. He was holding Jessie's hand, grinning at the camera. At his side, Jessie wasn't grinning, though. Instead, she wore a distinct pout.

He pointed to the photo. "What a face! What were you thinking that day?"

Her eyes narrowed as she thought back over the past. "I was upset," she said finally. "You were going to junior high school, and I still had two years of elementary school left. You had walked me to school every day of my life until then. It was the first time I'd ever had to be away from you, and I remember thinking I wasn't going to be able to stand it." She traced a light finger over his grin. "You, on the other hand, look thrilled to be moving on."

"I couldn't have been too thrilled," he said honestly. "I hated it when we were separated."

There was a small, gentle silence. It should have been awkward, he thought, but it wasn't.

"Oh, Ryan." She sighed. "We used to be so close. What happened to us?"

"You abandoned me for a jock." He'd meant the words to come out lightly, but as he saw her face change, he realized he hadn't been entirely successful. He forced himself to smile. "And I made millions and found a woman who would have me."

"Dinner's ready." Finn, his household assistant, breezed into the room. "When do I get an introduction to this ravishing beauty, Ryan?"

Jessie smiled and put out a hand. She didn't seem at all fazed by the neon-pink streak that marched through Finn's blond hair, or the leather pants that looked as if they'd been painted on his skinny butt. As Finn shook her hand firmly, she asked, "Why? Are you going to take me away from him?"

"Oh, no, darling." Finn batted his eyelashes outrageously. "I just want to borrow some of your clothing if it's all as exquisite as this outfit." He ran a long, elegant finger down the sleeve of her silk blouse.

As she laughed, Finn tapped the face of his watch and made an expressive face at Ryan. "Five minutes or less. You know how peeved I get when you wait until the lettuce is soggy."

As he turned and marched back out of the room, Jessie caught Ryan's eye. "Where on earth did you find him?"

He shrugged, grinning. "Finn's unique, isn't he? His aunt was our housekeeper until four years ago, when she had to retire because of knee problems. Finn filled the housekeeping position temporarily and gradually I found out he's an excellent chef, as well as a slick hand on a computer. He does laundry and oversees the yard work— the all-purpose manservant, you could say. I don't know what I'd do without him." He sobered. "He was a rock when Wendy was killed. His partner died of AIDS complications just before I hired him, so he knew what I was going through."

"I like him," she said.

He nodded. "So do I. However, he'll become highly unlikable in a hurry if we don't get started on his dinner."

"We wouldn't want that."

She preceded him into the dining room, where Finn had set their places at right angles at one end of the dining table. There was a gas fire merrily blazing in the fireplace.

Fresh cymbidium orchids in a clear glass bowl with cracked crystal marbles graced the center of the table and silver candlesticks held white tapers that matched the flowers.

"This is lovely," she said. "You shouldn't have gone to so much trouble."

He couldn't help it, he had to laugh. "I didn't," he confessed. "All I did was give a few directions. Finn's the one with the vision."

"You know what I mean," she said.

He shrugged. "I wanted to make it special."

Her eyes were very dark and green. "Why?"

"We're about to begin a new chapter in both of our lives."

Her gaze was on the table now. "Yes. We are." She was silent until after their meals had been served.

After Finn left the room, he cleared his throat. "How long after the procedure will it be before you know whether it worked?"

"They'll be monitoring me with bloodwork every three days to see if something the nurse called my Beta count is rising. I gather it's a hormone. It should rise steadily, and when it's over two thousand they begin to relax. After six or seven weeks, the fertility center will send me back to my regular obstetrician for the rest of the pregnancy, barring any complications. Which I don't expect, of course."

"Okay." He made a production out of cutting the excellent marinated sirloin that Finn had set before him. "Let's do it."

And do it they did. He rose early the next Thursday morning and went to the fertility center, where a very efficient nurse handed him a specimen collection cup and ushered him into a room where apparently, legions of men just like him produced "specimens." The room contained what the nurse primly referred to as "visual aids," men's magazines and a video machine with a couple of porn flicks to choose from.

As he unzipped his pants, he knew a moment's nervous concern, probably shared by every other guy who'd ever stood in there alone, expected to perform on command. What if he couldn't...he'd never had any problem remotely resembling it before, but this was a lot of pressure...it didn't bear thinking about.

In the end, though, all he had to do was think of Jessie, and his body responded as it always did to thoughts of her. Did she truly understand how things would be between them when they married? Though he'd happily give her a room of her own, he intended that they would share a bed every night. He thought of the sound of her husky voice whispering into his ear, the way her green eyes sparkled when she teased him, the clean, fresh scent of her hair and the way it felt like cool silk beneath his fingers, the feel of her soft flesh as he pulled her against him and drew her under him the way he'd dreamed of doing for years. Soon it would be *her* hands on him, exploring, stroking, guiding him to the hidden, humid center of her body....

As he repeated the same thing the following day, he mentally crossed his fingers as he washed his hands and his breathing slowed and calmed. If this clinical, somewhat humiliating process worked, he thought, tucking his shirt back into his pants and shrugging into his jacket, soon he'd be marrying Jessie.

She hadn't wanted him to stick around during her procedure, but he called her that evening. "Everything go okay today?"

"It went fine. Now all we have to do is wait."

"Do you have any restrictions?"

"No," she said. "They had me lie still for about ten minutes afterward, and that was it."

"That was it? Ten minutes? Hardly seems like enough time for my little swimmers to start fighting their way upstream."

She laughed, as he'd intended, and the constraint in her tone eased. "They have a powerful incentive, though."

The days dragged as she waited until she could ascertain whether she'd achieved her goal. Several evenings later she picked up a folder she'd brought home from the gallery and made herself go through the invoices, recording information on her laptop computer as she prepared the accounts payable. Working in the evenings kept her from pacing around the condo wondering if she was pregnant.

But halfway through the pile, she found a misfiled sheet of paper. It was short and to the point, and she could have recited it with her eyes closed. It was from the bank to which she'd applied for a loan. "We regret to inform you that your application for the following loan has been declined."

Suppressing the very unladylike words that clamored to be said, she set the sheet aside. She'd been sure she would qualify for that loan, and to learn that she'd been denied had been a setback she hadn't anticipated. When she'd called, Mr. Brockhiser had told her that their loan committee wasn't comfortable with her debt-to-income ratio. End of discussion. Still, there were other banks in Boston. She'd already applied to another one; perhaps they'd look more favorably on her.

Just then someone knocked on the door. She leaped for

it, knowing it was Ryan. He'd offered to drop by with dinner.

"Hi." He carried a bag from the deli down the street.

"Here." She handed him a small envelope, at which he stared.

"What's this?"

"A key." She avoided his questioning gaze. "I thought you might like to have a key to my place...since we're...you know."

He laughed. "Yeah. Whatever we are." He pocketed the key. "Thanks." Then he walked to the table and set out the sandwiches and cookies he'd bought. "Dinner arrives."

"Thanks." She indicated the sandwiches. "Which one do you want?"

"Either. I know you like seafood salad but if you don't want that one, I'll take it and you can have the turkey."

She reached for the seafood salad sandwich. "You're a prince."

"So they tell me." He took a bite of his own sandwich, then said, "We need drinks," and vanished in the direction of her kitchen. When he returned with two glasses of water, he said, "So how long do you have to wait now to find out if this worked?"

"About ten more days. My Beta count is rising but it's too early to tell."

He nodded, but she could see the excitement lurking in his eyes. He was as impatient as she was. "Would you like to go down to Chinatown this weekend? They celebrate the Chinese New Year."

"That sounds like fun. I've always wanted to do that."

"You never have? You'll love it," he predicted. "There's a parade, and they have dances with dragons and lions, and firecrackers. And we can have dinner at the New Shanghai.''

"I've heard it's fabulous."

"It is. Wendy used to love it. She always had the sliced lamb with scallions.''

Wendy. Again. Was it disloyal to wish her former friend wasn't included in every conversation they had?

Probably. And selfish, too. But still...if they were going to marry, *she* would be his wife soon. Would he continue to talk about Wendy then?

She forced herself to smile at him. "Sounds fabulous," she said. "I'll put Saturday night on my calendar."

The week passed surprisingly quickly, and before she knew it, their date was upon her. Dressing snugly to combat the chilly winter weather, she was just digging her gloves out of her dress coat pockets when the doorbell rang.

She walked to get it, puzzled. "Why didn't you just come in?" she asked when she opened the door to find Ryan standing there. "I gave you a key, remember?''

"I know." He shrugged. "It just seemed a little... presumptuous to walk in.''

She reached up and patted his cheek. "That's thoughtful. But feel free to walk in anytime.''

He took her wrist, holding it against his cheek when she would have dropped her hand. "Anytime?"

The look in his eyes was surprisingly intimate, and immediately her mind flashed back to his words from the night they'd discussed marriage. *Passion, I can promise you.* She cleared her throat as a jolt of pure sexual electricity shot through her. "Sure. Any friend of mine is welcome anytime," she said, trying to emphasize the friendship they'd agreed on. She wasn't sure she was very successful, though, since it came out as a croak.

He lifted her wrist to his mouth, and her eyelids fluttered closed as she felt his hot breath sear her tender flesh. Then his lips were on her, lightly pressing a kiss to the sensitive spot at the base of her hand, and she shivered as a knot of quivering nerves drew taut in her abdomen.

"What are you doing?" she managed.

He looked at her over the hand he still had pressed to his mouth, and his blue eyes were full of a triumphant mischief. "Seeing how you taste. Why?"

"I—nothing." She yanked her hand back, too flustered to pretend the caress hadn't scrambled her brain cells. Her skin tingled all over. "I thought we agreed to…to…to be friends."

"That was friendly." His tone was innocent.

She flung her bag over her shoulder and marched toward the door, unnerved by the sexual vibrations zinging around her small condo. "Hah."

"It wasn't *un*friendly," he pointed out.

"No, it certainly wasn't," she grumbled under her breath. Darn him! How were they supposed to keep their friendship the way it had been when he did sneaky things like that?

He didn't say anything else, but he whistled as they rode down to Chinatown, and when she glanced over at him, a small smile played around the corners of his lips.

The Chinese New Year's parade and celebration was noisy and bright and exuberant, and by the time the last float had gone by and the last firecracker had exploded in a shower of brilliant color, Jessie forgot she'd been annoyed with him earlier. From where they'd parked they walked down Hudson Street to New Shanghai and were seated moments after Ryan identified himself.

The room in which they sat was pretty and airy, its white linens giving it a more formal look than most of the local Chinese eateries. Ryan ordered the evening's special, a plate of baby eels glazed in a hot pepper and orange sauce, while Jessie stuck to a more mundane vegetarian entree.

"Uck! How can you *eat* those?" she said when the waiter departed.

He grinned. "Easily. Watch."

She grimaced again as he swallowed a spicy bite. "Gross. You always were a more adventurous eater than I was."

He laughed. "I'm a more adventurous eater than most of the known world. Mom always said I'd eat anything that wasn't nailed down."

The words brought a wave of unexpected nostalgia sweeping through her so strongly that tears stung the backs of her eyes. "How did you bear losing them?" she blurted out. "If they'd been my parents, I'd still be devastated."

Ryan's eyes grew shadowed, and for one brief moment she caught a glimpse of the grief that would always be with him. "We had a wonderful life together," he said quietly, "and I don't think they had any regrets. I miss them every day and, yeah, I wish they'd lived longer, but the memories are so good..." He trailed off, then spoke again after a moment of reflection. "What do you remember best about them?"

"That's easy." She sensed his unspoken need to gather memories of his family. In fact, she shared it. It was one of the most seductive things about their relationship, in some way, that they shared so much history. "Your mom was such a good cook. I remember she could hardly wait for the Michigan cherries to come in each summer. As soon as she got some, she'd bake pies and cobbler. She let me help, and it's still one of the few things I truly love to do in the kitchen.''

He was smiling now, his gaze faraway. "I'd forgotten about the cherries. That woman did love cherries.'' He reached across the table and squeezed her hand, then lightly linked their fingers and held the connection. "Thank you.''

"You're welcome. Hmm. What do I remember best about your dad?'' she mused. "I remember how he would toss me up in the air and catch me again, and the smell of his pipe when he sat on the porch with your mother on summer nights while we caught fireflies. I remember how, after he'd been fooling around in the car engine he'd come after us with greasy hands, pretending to be a monster.'' She shook her head. "I used to wish he was *my* father, because I thought there wasn't a more wonderful dad in the world than Mr. Shaughnessy.''

Ryan had been chuckling, but his laughter faded at her last words. "Jess—''

"Do you know,'' she said, "I have more vivid memories of *your* family than I do my own? That's sad.''

"It *is* sad,'' he said, "but look what you've become. I've always been amazed that your childhood didn't squelch your drive and determination. And it's another reason why I think we should marry. We share memories. We *know* how to make a child feel loved, how to give it security and a warm family atmosphere.''

She nodded. "You're right. I never realized where I got my ideas about being a mother, but you and I both know they didn't come from my mother.'' She thought bitterly of the way her mother had simply faded out of the picture when Jessie's grandmother had caught Jessie in some, usually minor, misdeed. If there had ever been a time when her mother had intervened while her grandmother was administering a "whipping" with the yard-stick, she couldn't remember it. "I'll never, *ever* hit my kids," she said suddenly, fiercely.

"I know." His fingers squeezed hers again, gently. "You're going to be a great mother. *We* are going to be great parents."

His words echoed in her head, driving home the enormity of the decision they had made in a way nothing had before. *We.* It was going to take some getting used to, thinking of herself as half of a pair.

She was pregnant!

At the end of the third week, the longest weeks of her life, another blood test confirmed her Beta count had risen sufficiently to make pregnancy a real possibility. And her period was eight days late. She was *never* late. Jessie wanted to dance around the room, but she was afraid to bounce her uterus around like that. Although the doctor had assured her this should be as normal a pregnancy as any other from this point forward, she figured there was no sense in taking chances.

A baby. She felt her eyes misting. She hadn't realized exactly how much she'd wanted this. It was hard to take in. She couldn't wait to tell Ryan!

She walked out of the clinic to her car, but as she climbed in and reached for her cell phone, she realized her hands were shaking. Carefully she dialed his office number, and when an automated voice picked up, she punched the sequence for his private line.

"Hello?" His deep voice made her heart leap.

"Hi, there."

He laughed, and she could imagine him relaxing, spinning his chair around to look out the plate glass window over the Boston cityscape. He would have the sleeves of his shirt rolled up and the knot in his tie probably had been loosened an hour or so after he got into his office.

"Well, hello." His voice warmed when he recognized her voice. "What are you up to today?"

"Guess." She worked hard to keep her voice level.

"Uh…" Apparently she'd interrupted him in the middle of some deep thought, because he didn't get it. "Give me a hint."

"I had a doctor's appointment today."

"Jess!" She had his full attention now. His voice rose as he said, "Are we going to be parents?"

"I'm almost positive." She didn't bother to hide her delight. "My counts are rising, and all the signs are positive."

"God, Jess…" He sounded a little dazed. "That's *great*."

"I know. I can hardly believe it! Oh, Ryan, I'm so excited."

"I know the feeling." His voice became jubilant. Then he grew quiet. "I wish I was there to celebrate with you."

I wish you were, too. Sternly she reminded herself that this wasn't a normal arrangement. She had no reason to expect him to be glued to her side. "It's okay," she forced herself to say calmly. "We'll celebrate tonight."

"We should go out for dinner," he said. "Do something special." There was a loaded pause. "Does this mean we can get married now?"

She was silent. Part of her wanted to shout, "Yes!" and she had to suppress the urge. His words reminded her of the reason they'd discussed marriage in the first place. Quietly she said, "In twelve weeks, remember?"

"Right." His voice was a little subdued now, too. "I guess I'll see you tonight."

They said goodbye, and she slowly replaced the handset

on the base, wondering why she felt so let down. She was pregnant. She should be thrilled.

And she was, she assured herself stoutly. It was just that…in the past two weeks things had changed between Ryan and her. They'd grown closer in a different way, a warmer, more affectionate way. It had been all too easy to forget that they were together because they each wanted a child. Too easy, she thought, to pretend that they were a normal couple falling in love.

They'd gone out several more times after the Chinatown trip, and though he hadn't kissed her, Ryan had held her hand, wrapped one hard arm around her back and touched her frequently. So frequently that she'd spent half their time together listing all the reasons it would be inappropriate for her to throw herself into his arms and beg him to kiss her.

He made it all too easy to pretend that love was a part of what was growing between them, with his solicitous attentions, the warm light in his eyes when he looked at her and the interest he displayed in every word she said.

Later that afternoon a large bouquet of pink and blue flowers were delivered to the shop. A small teddy bear on a stick was stuck into the middle of the arrangement, and two baby balloons danced gaily above the blossoms. Fortunately she was alone because Penny would have had a million questions and Jessie probably would have wound up telling her what was going on.

She couldn't keep herself from smiling as she detached the card and took it out of the small envelope. In bold block letters, Ryan had written: *Thank you for making my dream come true.*

She stared at the card. It would be easy to misinterpret those words, she thought as her heart beat faster. But he hadn't meant them in a romantic way. She was indeed making his dream come true: by giving him the child for which he'd always longed. And the sentiment on that card only acknowledged her part in that.

"Thank you for the flowers," she said when he arrived to take her to dinner that evening. She indicated the sizable bouquet in the middle of her small dining table.

He grinned. "I thought it was appropriate." Then he came toward her, gathering her into his arms and hugging her hard, lifting her feet clear of the floor. "This is going to be so great!"

She nodded, struggling free of his arms as her pulse raced. He used every opportunity to touch her, it seemed, and though he acted completely unaffected and innocent, she was sure he was doing it on purpose. It just wasn't fair of him to touch her like that, she thought. In the circle of his arms it was too easy to forget their arrangement.

Four

———

Three weeks passed.

One morning Jessie sat in her office with the door closed and a scowl on her face as she reviewed the contents of her latest rejection by the venerated monetary institutions of Massachusetts. Her loan application had been denied by the second bank with a speed that was less than flattering; a third bank informed her that they weren't taking on any new business loans for at least the next six months. Glumly she licked the flap of the envelope that held yet another application. Sooner or later she'd get lucky.

She'd better.

In the past few days she had investigated other avenues, but the interest rates at loan companies were staggering, and she knew better than to even consider it. In the meantime, her competitor had held a grand opening of their new, expanded store and she actually had customers who had the nerve to exclaim to her how wonderful it was. Grr-r-r-r.

And to top it off, she thought, as she hit the print button on her computer that would start payroll checks, she felt lousy. She'd been too queasy to eat breakfast every day for the past week. By midmorning, she was able to keep down a few dry crackers, and she was guzzling diet, caffeine-free soda which seemed to calm her stomach a little, but she was picking at lunch and dinner. Nothing appealed to her.

And she was tired. In the mornings she dragged herself around the store. Every day it was a fight not to simply lay her head on her desk and take a short snooze in early afternoon.

Ryan had been away for much of the past week on an extended business trip to the Northwest and he expected to be gone for at least another ten days. Though he called nearly every evening, she hadn't told him how she was feeling. It probably would pass by the time he returned.

Jessie finished the last of her decaf tea and set her mug in the dishwasher, then wound her scarf around her neck as she prepared to brave the icy morning. It was ridiculous for her to be missing Ryan. In the past she'd seen him exactly once a month. Once or twice a year there'd been a chance meeting at an art gallery opening, a charity event, a Pops or Boston Symphony Orchestra opening night. She'd nearly always had a date, and he'd been with Wendy. Their contact had been a casual moment of conversation at intermission or a wave across a ballroom.

No, she shouldn't be missing him. Wouldn't be, either, under normal circumstances, she assured herself. But nothing was normal right now.

As she walked briskly down the street to the gallery, hoping to settle her stomach, she prayed for a better day today. She hadn't dared to put anything more than tea in it this morning. Yesterday her queasiness hadn't been confined to breakfast but had lasted nearly the whole day. She had barely been able to tolerate the odor of her assistant's Reuben sandwich at lunch, and dinner, at which she'd met two other women who owned small local specialty shops, had been a disaster. She'd wound up in the bathroom on the verge of losing what little she'd been able to put in it.

She'd pleaded the flu to her friends and staggered homeward. Once she was in a horizontal position, she'd felt much better. But she could hardly spend her workday horizontal. As she arrived and began the process of opening the store, she took slow, deep breaths. She had too much to do to worry about a little morning sickness.

By lunchtime, though, she was barely holding on. Penny, her assistant manager, kept fluttering back and forth between the shop and the storeroom, where Jessie was sitting on a packing crate with her head resting against her coat, which was hung on the wall beside her.

"Gawd, Jess, you look *awful!* Maybe you should just go on home and rest. If this is the flu, I don't want it."

Jessie made a face at her. "Thanks, Pen. I can always count on you to know just the right thing to say."

Unrepentant, Penny giggled. "Sorry. But I'm *serious!* Nobody wants to feel like you obviously feel."

"You're right. I'd better just go home." She latched on to the excuse gratefully. She didn't want to tell anyone about this pregnancy until she was sure it was a go. "Why don't you see if Melissa can come in today and tomorrow?"

Penny nodded and scurried off to call Melissa. Then, before Jessie could catch her, she'd hailed a cab.

"It's only a few blocks," Jessie told her.

"A few blocks too many when you feel like that," Penny countered, giving the cabby a generous tip to make up for the short trip.

At home, she slept for several hours. *Good grief, Charlie Brown,* she admonished herself. She'd read about the difficulties that many women encountered during the early weeks of pregnancy. She'd thought she was prepared, but this unrelenting nausea was worse than anything she'd ever experienced.

Much to her dismay, the next week was no better. She went to work, but several times she actually had had to lie down on the floor in the stockroom. Even water made her poor stomach rebel.

Penny was worried sick. She alternated between tender solicitude and keeping a cautious distance until finally Jessie snapped, "For heaven's sake, Penny, it's not contagious. I'm just pregnant."

That, of course, had precipitated not only a shocked moment of silence but a million questions and oodles of sage advice—from a twenty-one-year-old whose closest encounter with pregnancy was once a year in the ob-gyn's office when she went for her annual female exam.

"Please," Jessie said as she crawled into yet another cab to go home scant hours after arriving at the gallery, "don't say anything to anybody, Pen. I don't want anyone to know just yet."

Penny nodded. "I understand. Now you just go home and rest. Don't worry about a *thing.* I'll schedule extra help for next week and make sure all our shipments come in."

She stepped back and closed the cab door after giving the cabby quick directions, and Jessie closed her eyes, hoping she could make it home without retching.

At home she lay down on the bed without even removing her clothes and fell asleep.

The next day was even worse. She could keep the nausea at bay only if she lay perfectly still. Even turning from one side to the other, made her head spin and her stomach lurch. Blindly she reached for the phone she'd set on the bedside table.

Her fumbling fingers knocked it to the floor.

Well, cuss. She had to call Penny and let her know she'd be late today. Carefully she turned her head just enough to see the clock on the nightstand. Eight-thirty. She was normally at the gallery by now, but Penny still wouldn't be there. She'd just close her eyes for a few minutes and try to call around nine….

The next time she surfaced, she forgot to be cautious. The moment she sat up and swung her feet to the floor she felt her stomach rebel. Cold sweat broke out all over her body as she quickly lay back down and took slow, deep breaths until she thought the danger was past.

She reached out a hand for the phone, but when her groping fingers encountered nothing but the clock, the lamp and the novel she'd been reading, she remembered she'd knocked it to the floor.

The floor. Okay, that wasn't so bad. Surely she could get the phone off the floor. She inched herself to the edge of the bed on her back, then reached down and flailed around. Her fingers just brushed the carpet. No phone.

Gingerly she began to move her head in small increments until she was looking sideways. Then, equally slowly, she rolled herself slightly to the side so that she could see the floor.

There it was! Half-hidden beneath the bed, but well within her grasp. Holding her breath, she made one quick lunge. Her fingers closed over the handset and she flopped onto her back on her pillow as another wave of nausea rolled through her. Success. With trembling fingers, she lifted it and punched the button she'd programmed for the shop, then lay listening to the ring as she willed herself to breathe and relax.

"The Reilly Gallery, Penny speaking. May I help you?"

"Hi, Pen."

"Jessie! I was *worried* when I got here and you weren't already around. If I hadn't heard from you by lunch, I was planning to come over and check on you. How are you feeling?"

She tried to chuckle, but even to her ears, it sounded a little weak. "Pretty rocky. Can you hold down the fort without me for a while?"

"Abso*lute*ly." Penny must've been a cheerleader in high school. Everything she said sounded like a pep talk. "Don't even *think* about coming in here today. Just rest and take it easy. Have you called the doctor?"

"No." She hated admitting that things weren't going well. But now she began to worry. What if there was something wrong?

The minute she punched the off button from speaking with Penny, she called the doctor's office. A cheery nurse fielded her call.

"Nausea is fairly common in the first trimester, Ms. Reilly."

"But this is…really bad."

"Perhaps you have a touch of the flu, as well. Have you been exposed?"

Of course she'd been exposed. She worked in retail, for heaven's sake. But all she said was, "Probably. Still, this doesn't seem like flu. I have no fever, and when I lie very still I feel all right. It's just when I move that I start to feel sick.''

"Morning sickness affects everyone differently," the nurse said confidently. "Once your hormone levels settle down, I'm betting you'll be feeling fine again."

"This isn't just a little morning sickness, though," she said anxiously.

"Sometimes it occurs in the evening. With a few unlucky ladies, it lasts all day. But it should begin to subside around twelve to fourteen weeks.''

Twelve to fourteen weeks! She was only working on her seventh. Quickly she did some mental math. Forty or so more days of this? No way. She'd be dead. When she said as much to the nurse, the perky voice laughed brightly.

"That's what they all say. But it'll pass. You wait and see." The woman went on to give her several suggestions for things that might settle her stomach. "If none of this works and you still are vomiting in a few days, call us again and we'll bring you in for an exam."

Days of this? The thought was too horrible to contemplate. She *had* to get over this! She couldn't afford to spend one day, much less twelve weeks or more, lying in bed watching the light shadows change on the ceiling.

This was ridiculous. She had to get something into her stomach. That probably was why she felt so awful. She always felt sick if she skipped a meal or waited too long to eat. She could control this. It was simply mind over matter.

But first…maybe she'd take a little nap. She had intended to try to go in to work but Penny's idea might be better. Rest, relax, try to eat right. Surely she'd feel better tomorrow.

But tomorrow came and the tomorrow after that and

yet a third one, and she still could barely manage to get around her apartment. By now she was counting days until she could call the doctor. The nurse had said a few days. Was three days a few? A week?

She wanted Ryan. It was irrational, she knew. They had made each other no pledges, merely contracted a marriage for some very tangible reasons. But still, she wanted him to hold her, to make her feel better.

But Ryan was away. And though he called her frequently, she didn't tell him how bad she felt. She didn't really know why. Was she afraid he would rush right home…or was she afraid he wouldn't?

She slept a lot. Penny came by each afternoon with updates on the gallery and got instructions. Jessie tried to eat, but even chicken broth and dry crackers wouldn't stay down. Trying to eat became such an ordeal that she simply didn't. Even sipping ice water was a risky proposition. By the following Monday, she was too tired and lethargic to dress. She called the doctor's office on the dot of 9:00 a.m. and got an afternoon appointment. How she intended to actually get there was anybody's guess, she thought, but she was going if she had to call for an ambulance and go in on a stretcher.

Ryan checked his watch at noon on Monday. He'd just climbed off a plane from Chicago and could hardly wait to see Jessie. He walked quickly to the bank of phones in the airport, wanting to hear her voice. She'd be at the shop.

But she wasn't.

"I'm sorry, Ms. Reilly is unavailable today. May I help you?"

"Tell her it's Ryan."

"I can't, sir. She's not in the gallery. Is this something

I could help you with? Or perhaps I could give her a message?"

"When will she be back?" She probably was out to lunch.

The woman on the other end of the line hesitated. "I can't say, sir."

There was a hint of something…worrisome in her tone. Alarm rushed through him. "What's wrong? Is she sick?"

"I—are you, uh, her significant other?"

He massaged the bridge of his nose. "I guess that's as good a description as any."

"Oh, good." Relief colored the youthful voice. "She's at home. If you want to talk to her, why don't you go by and see her?"

"Why isn't she in the shop?"

"I can't say, sir."

"All right, forget it. I'll go see her myself."

"Oh, good. That would be, like, *really* a good thing."

As he drove through the manic Boston traffic to Marlborough Street, he was aware of how tense he was. He purposely hadn't let her know he was coming home a few days early, so it was no one's fault but his own if she had lost the baby and he didn't know it.

Lost the baby. He knew that these early days of a pregnancy, whether a "high-tech" one or one conceived the old-fashioned way, could be tricky. He was conscious of a sick feeling in the pit of his stomach as he snagged a hard-to-get parking space in front of her Victorian brownstone and raced up to her apartment.

He rang the doorbell and waited. And waited…and waited. Impatiently he rapped on the door and rang the bell again. Finally, he opened it with the key she'd given him.

"Ryan!" Jessie stared at him.

He stared back. Clinging to the doorframe, she looked like absolute living hell. Dark circles ringed her eyes, and her bouncy dark hair lay flat and lifeless. There were hollows in her cheeks, and the sweatsuit she wore hung on her, clearly showing that she'd lost weight. "Did you lose the baby?" he demanded, anguish welling within him.

"No." Her voice was hoarse but her eyes went wide with shock. She made the smallest negative movement of her head. "I...I—excuse me." And she turned and bolted back down the hallway to her bathroom.

Too startled to catch her, he stared after her for a moment. She'd said she hadn't lost the baby. Then what...? And then he heard an unmistakable sound. Closing the front door, he quickly walked down the hall to the bathroom. The door had been pushed nearly closed, but it hadn't latched.

"Jess, I'm coming in."

"Don't!" But her voice lacked force, and he ignored her, shoving open the door and entering.

She half lay on the floor beside the toilet bowl. Her eyes were closed, and her face was white.

Without speaking, he flushed the toilet, then soaked a washcloth in cool water, wrung it out and knelt beside her. Gently he began wiping her face. "Is this morning sickness?"

She tried to smile. "No. It's more like every day, all day sickness."

He was appalled. "How long?"

"Over a week. First it was just mild nausea but it's gotten worse. It's a little better if I'm lying down."

"Okay." He set the washcloth aside and slipped his arms beneath her shoulderblades and knees, lifting her into his arms. She groaned and closed her eyes, but he wasn't worried. There couldn't possibly be much in her stomach to bring up. Leaving the bathroom, he walked down the hall to the bedroom and lay her on the wreckage of her bed. "Why didn't you tell me?"

She made a feeble motion with her hand, and her voice was fretful. "I didn't want to worry you."

Panic rose again. This couldn't be good for the baby. "Where's your phone?"

"Why?"

"I want to call the doctor," he said patiently. "This isn't normal."

"I already called," she said. "I have an appointment at three-thirty."

"I'll take you."

"All right. That would be…good." Her passivity was frightening, simply because it was so unlike her. He glanced at his watch. It was just after two. No sense in waiting until three-thirty.

"Can I bring you anything?" he asked.

"A settled stomach."

He chuckled because she expected him to. "Sorry, that's on back order." He tugged the mess of covers she'd twisted to the foot of the bed, straightened the sheet beneath her as best he could, then gently covered her with the sheets and blankets. Her eyes were closed; she appeared to be dozing.

Reaching for the phone he called the doctor's number. A woman with a cheery voice answered and tried to put him off, but he insisted. "I'm bringing her right in or taking her to the hospital. Your choice."

"All right," she said. "I guess we'll try to work her in early."

"No," he said. "Don't try. Do it. We'll be there in fifteen minutes."

The doctor's office wasn't far. Going back into the bedroom, he shook out a large quilt. Pulling back Jessie's blankets, he wrapped her in the quilt despite her feeble struggles and carried her down to the car. As a precaution he brought along the plastic wastebasket she indicated beside the bed.

At the doctor's office he carried her straight up to the desk and demanded that they find a place where he could lay her down. After taking one quick look at Jessie, a nurse showed them into an examining room with a vinyl exam table. "Lay her here," she said. "I'll get the doctor as soon as I can."

Once the doctor came in, things began to move.

"She's going to need to be admitted to the hospital for a few days," the doctor told him. "She's dehydrated. We'll put her on an IV to get some fluids into her, and I'll give her something for the nausea, as well."

"It won't hurt the baby?"

The doctor shook his head. "No. The biggest danger to the baby right now is the dehydration."

Six hours later she claimed she was beginning to feel better. She actually lifted her head from the pillow in the private room he'd secured and looked around.

"The hospital," she said in disgust. "I don't have time for this."

"You don't have a choice." Ryan straightened from the windowsill where he'd been reading the paper while she napped.

Her eyes were wide and sad. "This isn't how I envisioned spending my pregnancy," she said. "What am I going to do about the gallery?"

"Don't you have an assistant who could handle things temporarily?"

"Yes, but she's young and not very experienced." She

was clearly fretting. "I can't afford to have anything happen to my shop."

"All right," he soothed. "I'll go by and see how things are doing tomorrow. If there are any problems, I'll make sure they get straightened out."

"What do you know about running a gallery?" she asked in a mournful tone.

"Nothing." His made his voice cheery so she'd smile. "But I'll figure it out. I do know a few things about money, you know."

"I know." Her lips curved the slightest bit, and her words were slurred. "I suppose if you can do for the gallery what you've done for yourself I shouldn't complain. Maybe I should send *you* in to try to get me a loan."

"You're applying for a loan? Why?"

"I want to expand. Remember I told you I had competition?"

He nodded, recalling the conversation. "Yes. Expansion is a good decision."

"Tell that to the banks," she muttered.

His nose for business smelled trouble. "You've approached a bank?"

She nodded faintly. "Approached and been sent packing. By three so far. I'm in a risky business, apparently."

He snorted. "That's ridiculous. Bank boards can be so shortsighted." He took her hand and smoothed his thumb over her knuckles as her eyes drooped. "Stop worrying. I'll make you the loan."

"No!" Her eyes flew wide open. "Under absolutely no circumstance will I borrow money from you."

"It wouldn't be a crime, you know," he said testily. "I wouldn't be where I am today if someone hadn't helped me."

"I said no. Ryan, I'm serious. I want to handle it my own way!"

"All right, all right." He put his hands against her shoulders and pressed her back in the bed as she struggled to sit up. "I'll keep my nose out of your business."

She closed her eyes then, and he didn't speak anymore. Sleep—and fluids—were the best thing for her right now. Especially if they could control the unrelenting nausea. Beneath the light hospital sheet, she looked even thinner. She hadn't been big to start with—she couldn't afford this.

Afford. The word reminded him of what she'd just said about her gallery. Didn't she realize that she wasn't going to have to worry about money as soon as they were married?

Probably not. They'd hardly spoken since they'd sealed their deal over dinner. There had been no discussions of finances, of household affairs or combining their lives. They hadn't even spoken much about the baby yet.

Leaving her a note on the rolling tray at her bedside, he left the hospital and retrieved his car. Might as well go see if there was anything at The Reilly Gallery that he needed to straighten out. The last thing he wanted was for Jessie to be worrying about her business, even if its success or failure was immaterial to her future.

It was dark outside the single window in her room when she awoke again. As she stirred, Ryan rose from the reclining visitor's chair and came to stand beside the bed.

"Hey," he said softly, putting a hand over hers where it lay at her side. "You've been sawing logs for a couple of hours now."

She turned her head, looking in vain for a clock. "What

time is it?'' Then it struck her that the nausea had sub-sided.

"Eight-thirty," he said. "They'll throw me out in thirty minutes."

"I feel better." Experimentally she lifted her head and looked from side to side. Her stomach felt a little jittery, but nothing like the rolling waves of sickness in which she'd been wallowing since last week. "Could you raise the head of the bed a little?" When they'd brought her in, they'd laid her down in a flat position, for which she'd been intensely grateful at the time.

Ryan moved a little and pushed the button, moving her into a slightly more upright position. "Too much?"

"No, just right." She turned her hand and clasped his. "Thank you."

"No problem. All I did was push the button."

"Not for that. For taking care of me."

"That's my job," he said softly. "You're carrying my baby, remember?"

"I remember." She swallowed the small pang of dis-appointment at his response. Of course that's why he was concerned. She could lose the baby. "Have you talked to the doctor?"

He nodded. "He wants to keep you for at least two days, give your system a chance to recover. Then he'll evaluate and decide what to do."

"What does that mean?" she asked apprehensively. "I've got to get back on my feet. I have to work."

Ryan shrugged. "You can ask him when you see him tomorrow. I'm just the messenger. Oh," he said, "you're scheduled for a sonogram in the morning."

A sonogram? She knew she'd have several eventually, but when she'd called to make the appointment for her first prenatal checkup—which wasn't until next week, come to think of it—they'd told her they probably wouldn't do one until eight weeks or so. Simply the way her doctor liked to do things, the nurse said.

"Why is he going to do a sonogram now?"

Ryan hesitated. "I think he wants to be sure the baby's okay. Apparently, dehydration can be a problem."

Dear heaven. She felt tears rising. What if something had happened to the baby because she hadn't insisted on seeing a doctor last week? "Oh, Ryan," she whispered, "I'm sorry."

"Hey." He squeezed her hand. "Let's not panic yet. He assured me it was just a precaution."

"Will you come with me when they do it?"

From the way his face lit up, she could see that she'd pleased him. "Of course."

The sonogram wasn't what she'd expected. It was far, far more. When the technician slapped a cold, tingly goo on her stomach and began to run the equipment, a little thing that looked almost like a shrimp swam into view. "There he is," said the woman. "Turning backflips, lively as you please."

Ryan was holding her hand. He increased the pressure until her hand hurt, but she barely noticed for the awed delight racing through her.

Then the technician said, "Uh-oh!"

"What?" Ryan spoke at the same time Jessie did, and her feelings mirrored the apprehension in his voice.

But the lab worker was laughing as she pointed to the screen. "Look."

As they watched, something flickered on the black-and-white screen behind and to one side of the shrimp. The technician moved the sonar wand to one side and suddenly, Jessie realized what she was seeing. "There's another one!"

"Twins?" Ryan sounded shocked.

"You bet." The technician was grinning. "Two of the little guys in there doing the backstroke. Congratulations times two!"

"Twins." Jessie said, echoing Ryan. Did her face hold the same stunned expression of shock that Ryan's did? "I never dreamed there would be more than one."

"I take it you two weren't in treatment for infertility," the technician said. "We see a fair number of in-vitro moms in here with multiples." Then she pointed to the screen again. "But those siblings usually are fraternal. You know, from multiple eggs being fertilized. It looks like these two little ones share a single placenta. So you're going to have identical babies."

Later, after Jessie had been transferred back to the bed in her hospital room, they stared at each other. "Twins," she said. "I can't believe it." Her feelings were mixed. Having a child had been something she'd wanted so badly—but, she now realized, she'd wanted it on her terms. One baby, one easy pregnancy, nothing that would interfere too dramatically with her life and her work. Now here she was, stuck flat on her back in a hospital room, with a business that sorely needed her attention and not one but *two* babies growing inside her.

Two babies! The thrill that had come on the heels of the technician's words returned. If only she didn't have to worry about how she was going to manage two babies and expanding her gallery, she'd be ecstatic. Oh, Ryan's money could purchase the best in child care, she was sure. But then her babies would be taken care of by strangers. She wanted to care for them herself. In fact, she was a little shocked by the maternal possessiveness that seized her when she considered hiring help.

"I can't believe it, either." Ryan's response broke into

her chaotic thoughts. "There are no twins in my family. Are there in yours?"

The questions snapped her out of the fog she'd been in. "I don't know," she said slowly. "Nobody ever mentioned family. I don't even know if my grandparents had any relatives. My mother wasn't a twin—that I know of."

Ryan's eyes softened and she knew he was recalling her childhood. "Did they leave any personal papers or anything that might have family history?" Then he sat down beside her on the bed. "I don't suppose it matters, though. The reality is that we are going to be the parents of twins."

She gauged his expression. He didn't appear to be having any negative thoughts.

He stood up and began to walk around the small room. "When you get out of here, we'll get married. You can move in right away and then—"

"Whoa, horse," she said. "That wasn't the deal. We get married at the end of the first trimester."

Ryan looked impatient. "Why wait?"

She lifted her chin. "There are still eight weeks to go. Who knows what could happen. Hasn't this—" she waved wildly around the room "—taught you anything?"

His face was a thundercloud. "Nothing's going to happen."

"You don't know that."

He sighed, pushing back the sides of his suit jacket and stuffing his hands in his trouser pockets. "It just seems silly to wait. I hate the thought of people counting backward on their fingers to figure out which came first—the engagement or the embryo."

She almost laughed. But he was so serious. For the first time she realized how much the idea of having children out of wedlock bothered him. And it made her question the arbitrary time limit she'd set for this marriage. Was she *really* worried that something might happen to her baby? Babies, she corrected herself. No. This pregnancy might not be a laugh a minute so far but she had a good feeling about it.

So why was she really waiting? She'd accepted the idea of marriage, had even begun to look forward to creating a real family for her children. And then there were the other aspects of it—she was attracted to Ryan. She was *more* than attracted, if she could face the truth. His touch made her insides shiver. Just the memory of the way he'd said, "I can promise you passion," got her all hot and bothered and wondering exactly how it would be to share a bed with him, to run her hands over every hard, muscled inch—

"Are you ignoring me?" His voice sounded distinctly combative.

"No." She studied his face, dark brows drawn together, blue eyes glaring at her over that straight, uncompromising nose. He probably had shaved this morning, but already his jaw was shadowed with dark stubble that gave him a rakish look. "We can get married now if you like."

His expression changed to one of blank shock. "What? Why?"

She shrugged, smiling. "You're right. Nothing's going to happen. Why wait?"

He came toward her then, his eyes leaping with blue flame. "I'm not going to ask you if you're sure, because I'm afraid you'll say you're not." He sat on the edge of the bed and leaned toward her as she sat, mesmerized by the look in his eye. He cradled her cheeks in his hands, his big fingers sliding into the silk of her freshly clean hair and cupping her skull. "Thank you," he murmured as his mouth brushed over hers.

She inhaled sharply at the first intimate contact. She was reclining against her pillows but she instinctively lifted her hands to his shoulders and his lips settled onto hers as easily as if he'd done this a million times. He tested and tasted her, gently molding her lips with the warm, supple pressure of his, his tongue flicking at the corners of her mouth. She shuddered beneath the sensual onslaught, and a small moan escaped from deep in her throat. As the sound registered, he angled his head and parted her lips, sliding his tongue between her teeth to explore the moist depths of her mouth. She sank against him, forgetting everything but the magical sensations roaring through her at his touch—

"Whoops!" said a nurse's voice. "Looks like everything's fine in here!" A giggle faded as the door slowly closed, and Ryan lifted his mouth a fraction.

He was breathing heavily; she could feel her own heart pounding.

"Jess," he said in a deep, hoarse voice, "marriage is going to change our relationship. Are you ready for that?"

"Ryan," she said, equally seriously, "unless I'm mistaken, our relationship changed more in the last minute than it has in twenty-some years."

He chuckled, and his breath was hot and sweet on her face. "You don't hear me complaining." Dipping his head, he pressed one brief kiss to her lips, then gently took his hands from her face, letting her hair slip through his fingers. "I have to leave now. In the morning I'll make arrangements for a ceremony. Do you want a church? A minister? Justice of the peace? As long as we're married, I don't care how."

"I don't care, either," she said. "I know you'd like to get it done, so whatever's fastest is fine."

"If you weren't in that hospital bed, I'd be glad to show

you fast,'' he said, and she shivered at the blatant sensuality glowing in his intense gaze. Then he touched her lips with one long, blunt finger and swung out of the room, leaving her shocked at his frankness, flustered at the thought that they might be married in just a few days, and aching for him to touch her again.

Five

Just before noon the next day the door to Jessie's hospital room opened and Ryan came in. He had a large white box tied with pink and blue ribbon beneath one arm and as he came toward her, he set it on the bottom of the bed.

"Hey, there," he said. He loomed over her and caught her chin in one hand, kissing her briefly. "How are you feeling today?"

"Good." She wished he'd lingered over that kiss the way he had last night. The thought had her clearing her throat. When was she going to get used to his touch? This ridiculous meltdown of all her circuits that happened every time he put his hands on her had to stop. Concentrating on his question, she said, "They might take the IV out today. I'm actually having a soft diet for lunch."

He made a face. "Yuck."

She made a face at him. "It beats not eating anything."

"You have a point." He hitched up his suit pants and

sat on the edge of the bed, facing her. "I made some calls this morning. We could get married in two days."

"Two days!" She'd assumed there was a waiting period but apparently that wasn't so. "All right," she said cautiously. "I guess we might as well go ahead if I'm out of here by then."

He laughed. "Now that's what I call a ringing endorsement."

"It's just...I'm having a little difficulty keeping up with everything." She pleated the sheet with her fingers. "The doctor told me this morning that he wants to see how my body reacts when they take me off the antinausea drug. If I start to feel sick again, he'll prescribe something that should help, and I'll be able to go home." Then she sat up a little straighter. "What's happening at the gallery?"

"I just came from there. Penny and Melissa are working, and Penny has someone else named Jil on the schedule." He looked questioningly at her and she nodded, satisfied. Jil and Melissa were both part-timers who knew the merchandise and the artisans behind them well enough to speak with confidence. "Penny wanted me to tell you she sold four pieces of the Ramirez collection and one of the beaded crystal bags this morning and that sales have been steady."

"That's good news," she said. "Emanuel Ramirez is a Southwestern artist who designs silver jewelry. He's sent me some really stunning things."

"Where did you find him?"

"One of my friends was in Arizona and saw some of his work. She was so impressed she called me. She has a good eye and she's found successful items before, so I flew out and met Mr. Ramirez and brought back some samples to see how they'd do in Boston." She couldn't prevent the satisfied smile. "I can't keep the stuff in stock."

"You enjoy what you do." He was studying her face.

"I do. It's exciting to find new artists and new items that are unique. A lot of my clientele is tourists, of course, but I also have a growing number of people in the area who come in on a regular basis for wedding and birthday gifts. I've been thinking about looking for some distinctive baby gifts when I expand." She forced herself to ignore the little voice that said, *If you can get a loan.* "I think they would be a hit."

"Speaking of baby gifts," he said, reaching for the large box he'd brought in, "why don't you open this?"

"What is it?"

He shrugged. "I thought the first gifts our babies received should come from me."

Working the ribbon over one corner she slipped the lid off the box. Clouds of pink and blue tissue obscured whatever was inside. Carefully she lifted the tissue out of the way. Two stuffed toys, white tiger cubs with wide blue eyes, were nestled side by side in the remaining tissue. One was reclining; the other sat up. They had golden chains around their necks with faceted crystal hearts dangling from them.

She pulled them from the box and stroked the soft fur. "They're adorable," she said. "We'll keep one in each crib. They can watch over the babies for us."

He smiled indulgently. "There's something else in there."

Her senses went on red alert at the tone in his voice. Slowly, she set the stuffed animals to one side and reached back into the tissue. Her seeking fingers found a small box, and she withdrew it from the larger container. "Ryan, if this is what I think it is, you don't have to—"

"Shh." He laid his finger against her lips. "You know me well enough to know that nobody makes me do anything I don't want to, Jess. Just open it."

The little box was wrapped in glittering gold paper with a white bow. She tore away the wrapping to expose a black velvet box. Slowly, she exerted the pressure necessary to flip open the hinged lid. The ring inside was as spectacular as she'd feared.

It was composed of diamonds, one very large round-cut center stone with four small diamonds lining the band on each side. It was beautifully, classically cut and the stones caught the lights and shot shining sparks in all directions as she tilted it from side to side. "Ryan, this is incredibly lovely," she said. She intended to add that she couldn't keep it, but he forestalled her with a gentle hand over her mouth.

"Thank you, Ryan," he said. "I'll cherish it forever."

Her breath huffed out in a chuckle beneath his hand before he withdrew it. "But I can't accept it," she said seriously.

"Of course you can." His eyes were a deep sapphire today and they pinned her beneath a level stare. "You're going to be my wife, the mother of my children. Someday you can pass this ring down to one of our children." He leaned forward and took her upper arms in a light grasp. "Do you have any idea how happy you're making me?" His voice was intense, his eyes more so.

She hesitated.

"Please, Jess," he said, "don't make too much of this. You're beautiful. I want to give you beautiful things." Gently he took the ring from her and slipped it onto her finger.

"You think I'm...beautiful?" She had to clear her throat. "I thought you'd see me forever as the skinny, knock-kneed little kid who drove you crazy following you and Emily Preswick around when you were twelve and I was ten.''

He smiled. ''You were a pain in the butt that year, I'll grant you. But yes, I do think you're lovely.'' His smile faded and he brushed her cheek with surprisingly tender fingers. ''Your skin feels like silk to my touch. You have roses in your cheeks again and your eyes are sparkling. Your lips…'' His voice faded.

She shivered. He was looking at her mouth now and there was no mistaking the expression on his face. Slowly he leaned forward, cupping a hand around the back of her neck and drawing her to him as he set his lips on hers.

He wasn't tentative this time, though his mouth was gentle. Seductive. Warm and firm on hers, growing hotter and bolder, sweeping aside all her rational objections. He slipped his free hand around her back and pulled her against his chest, and her pulse leaped as her body, clad only in the silky pajama top he'd brought her from home, met the broad planes of his chest.

Her hands came up, clasping the heavy muscles of his shoulders, and he parted her lips, his tongue dipping deliciously deep, sweeping exploratory circles in her mouth until she met and answered his demand with forays of her own. His hand slid from the back of her neck to circle the base of her throat, and her pulse leaped as her breasts tightened in sensual hunger. But he didn't touch her there, didn't move his hand lower. He merely brushed his thumb against the racing pulse in her neck, over and over again, as he thrust his tongue into her in a shockingly intimate imitation of lovemaking.

Finally, he tore his mouth free, sliding it down her throat to nibble a path across her collarbone. ''Jess,'' he murmured against her skin. ''I want you.''

"I know." Her fingers were in his hair, caressing the silky strands. "This seems so odd."

"Not to me." He drew back, then stroked his palms from her shoulders to her elbows and back, slowly savoring the soft flesh with an absorbed look on his face. "What could be better than marrying your best friend, with whom you just happen to share incredibly hot sex?"

"We aren't," she reminded him.

"Yet." He sounded confident. "We will. And it will be hot enough to blister the paint off the walls."

"Could get expensive." She deliberately reached for a lighter tone.

He grinned, making his dimples deepen and her stomach contract. "Good thing I've got that covered."

She was released early in the afternoon of the following day. Minus the IV *and* the nausea, courtesy of the prescription the doctor had already started. He'd instructed her to take it easy until her twelfth week, at which time they'd start easing her off the drug and see how she felt. When she'd ask him to define "easy," she was immediately sorry. No working. No extensive walking. No stairs. Let someone wait on you for a few weeks. Her mind had reeled at the implications of all the restrictions. Then he'd said, "No sexual relations." Ryan was in the room during the doctor's visit, and she hadn't been able to look at him, though she could feel her face burning. Could he possibly be feeling as chagrined and frustrated as she?

An orderly took her down to the entrance in a wheelchair, where Ryan was waiting in the sedate silver Mercedes in which she'd ridden before.

"Guess we're going to have to get some car seats for this buggy," he said as he helped her into the car. "Or get a minivan. They make them with child seats built in now.''

She grimaced. ''The ultimate family transportation. I vote for buying car seats.''

''Mr. Shaughnessy?'' A woman came out of the hospital, holding the white box that held the two tiger cub toys he'd brought Jessie, just as Ryan lowered himself into the car. ''Don't forget this.''

Jessie's breath caught in her throat. Not at the thought of forgetting the stuffed animals, but at the arrested expression on Ryan's face. Turning, she looked at the woman walking toward them. She was short, petite and blond. Wide blue eyes were fastened on Ryan's face and she was smiling...*she was Wendy.*

Oh, not really, but the hospital attendant walking toward them with the box looked enough like Ryan's deceased wife that the likeness would be hard to miss. She glanced back at Ryan and saw that he certainly hadn't missed it. On his lean face was acute anguish, a deep, soul-searing grief burning in his blue eyes.

''I'll just pop this in the back seat,'' said the Wendy look-alike, beaming.

Ryan cleared his throat. ''Um, thank you.'' He gripped the steering wheel as the young woman placed the box in the back seat, and Jessie could see the tips of his fingers were white with pressure.

''There you go. Good luck!'' She stepped back and closed the car door, waving before hurriedly retreating into the warmth of the hospital.

It was a gray, dreary day outside, and Jessie felt gray and dreary as well. She glanced across at Ryan as he drove. His profile was somber and a muscle ticked along his jaw. She opened her mouth, then closed it again. What was she going to say? He clearly didn't want to discuss it, or he'd have brought up the topic himself.

Holy cow! Did you notice how much that girl looked like my dead wife?

No. He obviously didn't want to talk.

Insecurity hunched her shoulders deep into her coat, and she turned her face to look out the passenger-side window as her eyes brimmed with sudden tears. She didn't have huge expectations for this marriage, she assured herself. As long as they remained friendly and got along well enough to be good parents, that would be sufficient. So what if they didn't have a great, all-consuming love like Ryan had apparently felt for Wendy? Might as well keep her track record intact. She'd never known the love that most people took for granted from the ones who shared their lives. Chip had been her only experience with love, and his affection had been cloying, his tendency to set her on a pedestal and cater to her stifling rather than inspiring love in return.

When he turned on Commonwealth Avenue heading away from the Commons, she came out of her silence. "We're going the wrong way."

"No, we're not." His voice was quiet and deliberate. "No exertion, remember? The doctor said you need someone with you for a while."

"That isn't exactly what he said—"

"So you can move in a few days early. When I'm busy, Finn will look after you."

"I don't need looking after." She made an effort to relax her gritted teeth. "I just need to be a little careful. I'd prefer to stay in my own place."

Ryan shook his head. "Not an option. If I go out of town, I want to know that you're not overdoing it or lying in bed too sick to move." His right hand left the wheel and settled briefly over her stomach. "I want to see these babies alive and well in seven or so more months."

So he only wanted to be sure she was all right because of the babies. "I'll hire someone to check on me daily," she said, mentally juggling her finances, knowing she really couldn't afford it.

He simply shook his head again and kept driving toward Brookline.

"I'm not ready to move in with you," she said, trying to keep the desperation out of her voice. Why did this bother her so much? How many women would object to living in a mansion like Ryan's? With Ryan to ice the cake.

"What difference does a few days make?" he asked in a voice that dripped with reason and made her long to punch him. "We're getting married as soon as you can stay on your feet for more than five minutes without wearing out. Are you telling me you weren't planning on living with me after we're married?"

"I haven't had time to plan anything!" she yelled.

There was a small silence in the car. Ryan braked at the tail end of a traffic snarl and laid his arm along the back of her seat, turning to face her. "I want you to live with me, Jessie," he said quietly. "I don't want this to be a marriage in name only or some weird kind of commuter marriage. I want my wife and my children in my house." He raked a hand through his hair and looked out the driver's-side window. "I guess there are a few things we need to talk about, aren't there?"

She nodded tightly.

"All right." He sighed, facing forward and releasing the brake as the traffic began to move sluggishly. "Will you at least rest awhile and have dinner with me? Then, if you really want to go home, I'll take you."

He sounded so reasonable that it would have been churlish to refuse. Even if she was dying to get back to her own home. "All right."

When they arrived at his house, Ryan helped her out of the car, then bent and lifted her into his arms before she realized what was happening. She gasped and clutched at his shoulders. "You're going to give yourself a hernia."

He chuckled as he carried her through the garden. "I've carried furniture that was heavier than you, cupcake."

"Cupcake?"

"Just a figure of speech." As he went up the steps and across the flagstones of the semicircular patio, the back door opened. "I've been expecting you, Jessie," Finn called from the doorway. "Welcome. I've prepared the most scrumptious chicken consommé for you and I have a room all ready—"

She caught Ryan's warning shake of the head and Finn stopped abruptly.

"It's all right," she told Finn. Without looking at Ryan, she said, "Actually, I am more worn out than I'd expected. I think I'd like to rest before I eat. Could you take me straight to the room?"

Without a word Finn turned and led the way through the house. Ryan carried her upstairs without even breathing heavily, and she caught herself wondering exactly how much exercise he got in a day's time. His upper chest and shoulder were a hard rock wall beneath her head, and she could feel the powerful flex of muscle in his upper back as he shifted her slightly.

The room into which Finn took them was absolutely beautiful. If she'd dreamed up the perfect environment for herself, it couldn't have been better. She loved pretty, feminine things, and this was the ultimate in both. The wallpaper was a muted pattern of pink and lavender flowers with a suggestion of soft-green leaves down to a chair rail, beneath which was a subdued pearl and lavender stripe. The sheer, filmy curtains over the shades echoed the same pearly shade and a swath of fabric that matched the flower wallpaper created a striking yet informal swag across the top and draping down the sides. A duvet in the same fabric was accented by silky pearl and lavender pillows as was the fabric covering a genteel lady's chair in one corner.

The bed itself looked like mahogany, as did all the furniture in the room, including a tall cabinet whose doors were folded back to display an up-to-date technological bonanza of computer equipment. As Ryan set her down on the edge of the bed, she noticed a small marble fountain with gleaming pebbles in it on a table against a wall, its small waterfall creating a pleasant, soothing sound. When Finn touched a button on the remote control that lay on the bedside table, a television screen unfolded from the ceiling into a not-quite-vertical position perfect for viewing from the bed.

"You can change the angle of the dangle, so to speak, with these," he said, chortling as he pointed to a couple of little, arrowed buttons. Then he set it down and walked to the right side of the room. Sweeping open a door, he touched a panel and illuminated the largest walk-in-closet she'd ever seen. "Voilà. Madam's wardrobe."

"Holy cow. I could live in there," she said. Her organized heart was singing as she looked at all the cedar shelves, vinyl zippered cupboards and hanging spaces for a wardrobe.

To the left of the closet, a pale-pink marble bathroom with gleaming brass accents was visible through a set of double doors. A large, freestanding glass shower stall rose in the middle of the room. Along one wall two wide steps led up to an enormous spa-tub with a tasteful collection of plants, candles and bath soaps ranged around its broad lip. The wall behind the tub was a thick, opaque window that let in the light without any danger of exposure to prying eyes. At one end of the tub, a television was built into the wall.

She walked slowly into the bathroom to get the full effect. His and hers sinks lined the wall opposite the tub; beside the tub, flames danced merrily in a small gas fireplace built into the wall. There was a separate, small stall with a toilet and bidet just inside her door. At the far end another set of double doors revealed a masculine suite.

"My rooms," Ryan said.

Wordlessly she turned and paced back into her bedroom. She sat carefully down on the side of the bed as both men stared at her. "What's wrong?"

"I've finally realized just how wealthy you really are," she said to Ryan. "It's a little…disconcerting."

He gave a snort of laughter. "Because I have a really cool bathroom?"

She shook her head and waved a hand to indicate the room. "It's everything." Then she hesitated, not knowing how to phrase the question burning in her brain. "Was this…?"

Ryan nodded. "Wendy's room. But Finn completely redecorated it when I told him we were getting married. New carpet, new furniture, new wallpaper and curtains—"

"The paint's not new," Finn said modestly. "I was afraid it would leave an odor and really, the paint was in fine shape. So I simply went for a look that blended with it. It wasn't difficult. There are some stunning fabrics and wallpapers out there. The furniture can be exchanged if you prefer a different style.''

''It's lovely,'' she said, smiling at Finn, hoping to mask her relief at not having to sleep in a bed that had belonged to Wendy. ''Really, really lovely.''

Finn blushed. ''We do our best.'' He turned and bustled to the door. ''I'm going to fix you a tray and bring it up. Then you can rest right here all afternoon.''

There was silence in his wake. The room seemed calmer, as if Finn stirred the very air around him. She glanced at Ryan and caught him grinning, and she couldn't prevent her own laughter from escaping. ''He's certainly…energetic.''

''He's manic,'' Ryan said. ''Give him a project and he works as hard as a squirrel on steroids. You have no idea how much fun he had with this. He did his own rooms, too. I asked him if he'd live in, and he agreed. So there will always be someone here for you when I'm not home.'' He hesitated, then walked toward her. ''Time for you to lie down. You're weaving.''

''I feel like a piece of well-cooked spaghetti,'' she complained. ''It's ridiculous.''

''You've been ill,'' he reminded her, ''*and* you're pregnant.'' He took her elbow, and she stood docilely while he pulled back the covers with the other hand. Then he bent and tugged off her fashionable boots, and when she lay down, he covered her with the duvet. ''I have some things to do. Let Finn feed you and then you can rest. I'll go by the gallery before it closes and see how everything's going.''

''Thank you.'' She laid her hand over his where it pressed into the bed beside her.

He smiled, bent and pressed a kiss to her forehead. ''No problem. Cupcake.''

She grimaced. "It's a good thing I don't have anything to throw at you."

He only laughed as he rose and walked from the room.

When Ryan got home that evening, Finn met him at the door. "She's still sleeping. I checked on her once each hour. After she ate a little soup, she crashed and burned."

Ryan nodded. "I don't think she realizes how weak she is right now." He set down the bag with the logo of a familiar department store, and Finn took his cashmere overcoat. "I'll be with her. Why don't you set dinner at that little table in my suite?"

Finn saluted with his free hand. "Aye-aye, cap'n."

He picked up the shopping bag and took the stairs two at a time, but when he got to the door to her room, he paused. The door was slightly ajar, and the new colors seemed wrong to him for a moment. He was used to seeing the cool blue-and-white scheme in which Wendy had decorated the room.

Wendy. He'd had a bad moment this afternoon when that nurse had walked toward him. Though she hadn't looked *that* much like Wendy, at first glance anyone could have been forgiven for mistaking them.

He didn't think Jessie had noticed the resemblance. She'd been very quiet on the way home, and he suspected she was fighting to stay awake. The doctor had warned them that sleepiness was a side effect of the medication she was taking.

At any rate, he'd spent the rest of the ride thinking about his life before Jessie. He'd been happy. Not delirious, but happy. Wendy had loved him totally, and his heart, bruised from years of longing for Jessie, had responded to her warmth and sweetness. And yet, if he were honest with himself, there had always been a small pocket inside him that had remained untouched. Waiting for Jessie.

He'd never in a million years have imagined this current scenario, and guilt streaked through him. Rationally he knew he hadn't wished Wendy's death. But it was hard to shake the feeling that he'd never been as good to her as she deserved.

Slowly he pushed the door wider so that he could see the bed. Jessie lay on her side, still sleeping. Her dark hair was tousled, and her face was peaceful, her lips slightly parted. One hand was tucked beneath her cheek, the other dangled over the side of the bed. Quietly he picked up a chair and set it beside her, then took her hand in his.

Her eyelids fluttered. The silvery-green gleam of her eyes appeared, and then she smiled at him, turning her hand in his and gently squeezing. "Hello."

"Hello." The moment was so sweet he thought his heart might burst. "I'm going to have to change your moniker to Sleeping Beauty."

She glanced beyond him to the window and he saw her eyes widen as she realized it was full dark outside. "What time is it? How long did I sleep?"

"About five hours," he said. "It's seven-thirty."

"Seven-thirty!" She pushed herself upright, tugging the sweater and slacks she'd worn home from the hospital into a wrinkled semblance of order.

He waited for her to protest, to demand that he take her home immediately. But all she said was, "Poor Finn. I didn't eat much of his lunch."

"It's all right," Ryan said. "He'll forgive you if you do justice to dinner. It's the same thing, by the way."

She made a face. "Tomorrow I'm allowed to eat more. You'd better warn Finn his consommé days are numbered."

He'd love to ignore the whole topic but he knew they had to talk about it. "Will you be here tomorrow?"

She hesitated, biting her lower lip. "I guess so." She looked up at him, and he couldn't resist laying his finger on the lip she was mutilating. She released it immediately and gave him a small, forlorn smile that quivered at the edges. "I don't know why I'm having such trouble with the concept of moving. I had expected to when we got married. It's just—I've had to look after myself for a long, long time. I feel odd letting someone else take over. It feels wrong, somehow."

Pity rose for the little girl who'd had to make her own school lunches, who'd often had so many chores she didn't have time to come out and play...the little girl who'd been alone long before her grandparents and her mother died, one by one, when she was in high school and college. He tended to forget the way she'd lived as a child. It would have destroyed a lesser person. But Jessie had drawn strength from somewhere inside herself and triumphed. No wonder she had trouble accepting help.

Quietly he said, "I don't want to take over, Jess. We're going to be a team. Right now we need to work out strategies to win in October." October sixteenth, the magic date. That was when the twins were due, although they'd been warned that multiples often came early.

"You're right," she said. "Accepting help will be my personal challenge." She took a deep breath. "Would it be okay with you if I stayed here tonight?"

His chest rose and fell in a deep sigh of relief. He supposed he'd better not tell her he'd been to her apartment and packed a small suitcase of things for her. "That would be more than okay," he said. "Tomorrow I'll bring you some of your things."

* * *

The next three days were quiet. He brought Jessie some clothing and her toiletries. Finn reported that she slept a great deal, though she stayed in close touch with Penny at the gallery. The doctor called on Thursday and sounded pleased when she reported that she was resting a lot and feeling much better. At night they discussed her gallery, his business dealings and read each other information from the dozens of baby books he brought home. It was extraordinarily satisfying in some ways, though he knew it was merely a lull in the action. Once Jessie began to feel better, she'd be chafing at the bit. And once the babies came…well, he couldn't even imagine it.

On Friday Ryan had appointments nonstop until three. Then he buzzed his secretary and told her to cancel everything for the rest of the day. As he'd promised Jessie, he took a pass by the gallery. Penny, the assistant manager, was young, but Jessie had chosen well and trained her even better. There was very little for him to do other than check the accounts and authorize a few payments on Jessie's behalf. Penny had even taken over the books.

When he got home, Finn didn't greet him at the door. He hung up his own coat, which was fine with him, though Finn usually insisted on doing his butler imitation, and headed through the house, wondering if Finn had gone out to the store or something. Then he heard the laughter.

He followed the sound upstairs to Jessie's room. As he neared the doorway, he heard her say, "Ha. *Q-U-E-E-N.* On a triple-word space, that's thirty and let's see, fifteen. Mark me down for forty-five points, Finn."

"You witch!" Ryan could barely understand the words because Finn was laughing so hard. He knew from experience that his employee considered himself a champion Scrabble player. "I swear those big numbers stuck to your fingers when you dipped into that bag. Rematch tomorrow." But humor colored his voice.

"You're on." Then she caught sight of Ryan lounging in the door. "Hi! Are you early? I just beat the pants off Finn."

"You won by three points," Finn said testily. "And only because I couldn't get rid of that *K* I drew near the end." He rose and turned to Ryan. "Sorry I didn't hear you come in."

Ryan shrugged. "Understandable. Nothing like getting beaten by a girl to make you concentrate."

"Hey!" Jessie shook a finger at him. "Chauvinism is uncalled for."

Finn glared at him. "I'd like to see you do better."

Ryan laughed. "You'd both clobber me. Numbers are my forte, not letters."

Finn and Jessie finished putting the game pieces in the box, and Finn rose from the chair he'd set at a small table beside the bed. He replaced the chair and table in their original positions and then took the game from Jessie. "I'd better get dinner started. How does a chicken casserole sound?"

"Great." As he left the room, she turned to Ryan. "He's a lot of fun. I could get used to lying around in the lap of luxury all day."

It shouldn't bother him that part of the reason Jessie was marrying him was because she knew he could provide for their children and her, he told himself. Hadn't he used his success as one of the lures when he'd been talking her into it? "Feel free to do that if it makes you happy," he said. " I don't care if you never work again."

Jessie looked horrified. "You may not, but I do. I've worked hard to turn The Reilly Gallery into something unique and special. It's more to me than just a job."

He nearly pointed out that she'd been more than happy to forget it for the past week, but his rational self reminded him that she'd been too ill to think much at all. What was the matter with him?

He was afraid he knew the answer to that. He had dreamed of Jessie for years, then given up that dream. Now suddenly the dream was tossed in his lap. Part of it, anyway. And though he anticipated the physical part of their new relationship with a need that was nearly painful, it wasn't enough. He wanted her to want him the way he wanted her. Not just physically but emotionally. He wanted her, body and soul. Heart and mind.

He wanted it all.

Six

The next day was Saturday.

Ryan knocked on the door of Jessie's room shortly after eight. She knew he'd already been up for an hour, working out in the weight room on the third floor.

"Come in," she called.

He turned the knob and pushed open the door, looping the white towel he carried around his neck. "Good morning. Shall I have Finn bring up some breakfast?"

Jessie pursed her lips. "I think I'd rather eat downstairs."

But he stepped forward before she could rise from the bed. "Uh, why don't you let Finn coddle you this morning? Save your energy."

"For what?" she asked with a wry grin. "My afternoon nap?"

"Well..." He walked to the bed and stood looking

down at her. "Actually, I thought we might go to a wedding today if it wouldn't tire you out too much."

Her eyes widened. "You mean *our* wedding? Get married today?"

He nodded. "No reason to wait, is there?"

She shrugged, shook her head. "No. There isn't." She squared her shoulders. "All right. Let's do it."

"Great." He turned and headed for the door. "I'll get Finn up here with breakfast, then he can lay out something for you to wear."

Two hours later she sat in a chair outside the office of the justice of the peace. Finn sat beside her while Ryan paced restlessly up and down the hall.

"You look lovely," Finn said. He fussed with the peek-a-boo lace across the bodice of the dressy suit she'd chosen. "That ivory suit was a wonderful choice."

She grinned at him, though her attention was still on her husband-to-be, who seemed far more nervous than he should, given the fact that *he'd* railroaded *her* into this marriage. "I never expected to wear this to my wedding when I bought it."

"Oh, dear heavens!" Finn sprang to his feet. "You don't have any flowers!" He zipped over to Ryan's side. "I'm going to get some flowers. You cannot get married without flowers."

"Get a camera, too," Ryan said. "One of those little disposable ones will do."

He caught her eye as Finn disappeared. "You heard the man. We *cannot* get married without flowers."

She chuckled. "Wanna bet?" Then she looked around. "It feels funny to be out in public again after feeling rotten for so long."

Ryan crossed to her side and took the seat Finn had vacated. He put his arm around her, hugging her close to his side. "You have no idea how relieved I am to see you feeling better."

"About as relieved as I am to be feeling better," she said. "When I scheduled this pregnancy, I didn't leave any flex time for problems like *this*. I've got to get back to work."

Ryan was silent for a moment. Then he said, "It's possible you're going to have to stick to a modified schedule for some time once you go back, you know."

"A modified schedule?" She didn't like the sound of that. Was Ryan going to be one of those husbands who wanted his wife at home? She thought he'd clearly understood her position on that the other day—

"Part-time," he said. "Until the doctor thinks you're really fit enough to handle a full schedule. Carrying two babies presents some extra difficulties sometimes."

"Once I get past this queasy stage, I'll be fine." She couldn't let herself believe otherwise. Her store *needed* her. And she needed it. She'd worked so hard to make her business what it was, to support herself, to be a success. If she didn't get back in there soon, all that would be in danger.

As she was mulling over the dark thoughts, Finn returned. He carried a bouquet of orange blossoms and made them pose for a ridiculous number of pictures on the small camera he'd bought while they waited.

Finally the doors to the justice of the peace's chamber opened. A beaming couple came out, holding hands, with several people behind them, and Jessie swallowed her nerves as Ryan took her hand and led her inside.

The ceremony didn't take long at all. Her hands shook as she placed the wedding band on Ryan's finger and accepted hers from him. His hands were cool and steady, and he put an arm around her as they spoke their vows.

When he kissed her, he kept it brief, but the telling pressure of his lips and a quick wisp of his tongue across her bottom lip turned her bones to jelly.

After the ceremony, she glanced up at him covertly. Could Ryan really be her husband now? He met her eyes and in his, she saw the warmth and reassurance she realized she'd craved. She'd been so afraid this was a mistake, so afraid Ryan would regret marrying her. So afraid he'd be thinking of Wendy today. But as they signed their names to the license, all she saw in his expression was pleasure and a confidence that steadied her. Finn snapped pictures and tossed a few handfuls of orange blossom over them as they exited the chamber. Then Ryan carried her back to the car and took her home to bed again.

Alone, as the doctor had ordered.

It was hardly the wedding day she'd hazily imagined when she'd allowed herself to consider that she might someday marry. But because it was Ryan who'd slid his ring onto her finger, it became the perfect wedding.

She went back to the doctor the following week.

As Ryan had predicted, she got edgier as she began to feel better. She'd begged him twice to take her down to the gallery "just for a quick look around," but he'd refused, telling her the doctor would let her know when she was allowed on her feet again.

She walked into the doctor's office, though Ryan had carried her out to the car, and he could feel her impatience with the restrictions.

"Well, hello," said the receptionist. "It's nice to see you in a vertical position today."

Jessie smiled. "I'm feeling much better."

When it was their turn, the doctor pronounced himself very pleased. He told her she could work three half days a week until he saw her again in two weeks, near the middle of March.

"But I feel fine now," Jessie said, clearly unhappy with the doctor's edict.

The obstetrician merely smiled. "I know. But I don't want you to overdo it. Once you've reached twelve weeks and we see how your body responds without any medication, we'll talk about working more."

As they got back into the car to go home, Jessie said glumly, "At this rate my store will be in the red by the end of the year."

"No way." He checked for traffic, then swung out onto the street. "Penny is doing a fine job. I haven't been lying to you."

"Yes, but I've already had to cancel appointments for a loan twice, and who knows when I'll be able to reschedule them?"

"You'll be back on your feet again before you know it. And I bet you'll have a loan soon thereafter."

She was silent. When he looked her way again, her lower lip was quivering.

"What's the matter?" He reviewed the conversation. What had he said? Done? The books weren't kidding when they said a woman's hormones went crazy during pregnancy.

Jessie took a deep breath and sniffed. "I feel superfluous. I'm not necessary to the gallery."

You're necessary to me. The words very nearly popped out of his mouth before he controlled the thought. "You're necessary," he said patiently. "Penny doesn't have the experience or the people skills to court your artisans. She doesn't begin to have your eye for striking displays and for what works with what. Sure, your products have continued to sell well, largely because they're unique, quality items that *you* selected." He took a breath. "You hired an efficient, organized assistant. Right now she's doing exactly what you need her to do. Soon you'll be able to do what you do best again. And once you do, that other shop will be sunk."

She didn't say anything, and her lip continued to quiver.

He didn't know what else he could say to make her feel better, so he concentrated on the traffic, feeling clumsy and awkward. He hoped he hadn't made her feel worse.

Finally she sighed. "I really hate to admit this, but I'm exhausted. I guess I'd better lie down again when we get home."

He smiled, relieved that she was recognizing her limits. "You did well today. Tomorrow you'll feel even better."

"Tomorrow," she said, "I'm going to work for a whole half day."

Three weeks later he took her to her apartment on Saturday morning. It was the first time she'd been in it since the day Ryan had taken her to the hospital. She knew he'd sent Finn over twice to clean it, and the bed had been neatly made with fresh sheets.

"Pack whatever you think you'll need for the short term," he told her. "Soon you're going to need new clothing, anyway."

She glanced down at her stomach. Although she didn't have anything to compare it to, she was pretty sure a pregnant mother of a single baby didn't look like she looked already. She was barely nine weeks and already none of her pants fit. "I'll put anything I think I can still use in one suitcase and pack the others for you to bring over when you can."

"Put a sign on anything you want to keep," he said. "The rest can either go into storage or I can arrange to have it sold."

"My lease isn't up until September," she said. "I'll put a sign on the things I want to take to your house and we'll leave the rest here. I'll have to sublet it, and it's easier if it's furnished."

"That's not a problem. I can take care of it for you."

"That's all right. I'll do it." She looked around. "I suppose there really isn't very much here that I want to take with me. I won't need furniture." She fished in her purse for her key ring and detached a key from it. "While I'm packing, you could go down to the storage room in the basement. Stacked against the left wall back toward the corner are three boxes of things I kept after my mother died."

"All right." He accepted the key, then took her by the hips and tugged her against him in one quick, unexpected move. "How about some incentive?"

Her heart skipped a beat. His body was hard and exciting against hers, throwing off a heat that nearly scorched her. Did he have any idea how much she wanted him? Tentatively she lifted her arms to his wide shoulders. "I could probably manage that."

He looked down at her, and his eyes shot a brilliant blue challenge. Suddenly she understood that look. He'd initiated the few kisses they'd shared. Now it was her turn.

Slowly she lifted herself on tiptoe. Dimly she realized she was shaking as she drew near his chiseled mouth—

And then she pressed her lips to his. His mouth was cool and firm, but it warmed, softened as she kissed him gently. His arms came around her and she slid hers up his neck into his hair. And the kiss caught fire. His mouth hardened, plundered. She gasped, and he used it to advantage, sliding his tongue deep inside her tender mouth, bending her back over one arm as she clutched at him for balance. He kissed her endlessly, then slid his mouth along her jaw to her earlobe, and she jerked in shock as she felt his teeth nibbling at the sensitive flesh. Lightning bolts of raw sexual need shot through her; she arched her back, pressing her lower body firmly against him. He was taut and hard and already aroused. Deep within her, an empty ache begged for his fulfillment.

But he was ending the moment, drawing back the slightest bit, his mouth leaving her ear. His breath was a hot rasp against her flesh as he lifted his mouth from her and set her upright again, and his kiss-reddened lips quirked at one corner.

"Whoa," he said, and his gaze was intense. "Guess you're sorry you started that."

Somehow she found her voice. "Not sorry. Only sorry that we can't finish it."

There was a full five seconds of silence as his eyes narrowed. "You picked a hell of a time to admit you want me."

She shrugged. "You picked a hell of a time to start something."

They stared at each other a moment, then a chuckle worked its way up through Ryan's chest, rolling out as a rich, sustained shout of laughter. "We're a pair," he said, releasing her and strolling to the door.

She stood in the middle of her apartment after he left, one hand pressed against her mouth. He hadn't touched her that way since she'd been in the hospital. Instead, he'd kissed her on the forehead, rubbed her shoulders and casually held her hand as if she were nothing more than a good friend.

Which she was, wasn't she? No, darn it, she was his

wife! And she wanted him to…to touch her as if she were more than just a friend.

She'd begun to wonder if he would lose interest as she grew rounder and less desirable. But that kiss! That kiss left her in no doubt that he was anticipating the day when the doctor gave her the green light to pursue normal activities.

The trouble was, making love with Ryan wasn't *normal,* for her! An involuntary shiver worked its way through her body, lingering deep in her abdomen. She wanted him, and he'd made it more than clear that he wanted her. But where did it go from there? Unhappily she walked into her bedroom and opened drawers, filling the first of her suitcases that Ryan had pulled out and laid open on the bed for her.

He was so very dear to her in so many ways. Not only did they have their childhood memories to draw them together, they had the friendship they'd established as adults. And now they had love.

Her hands stilled on the stack of sweaters she'd just set in the suitcase. No, she corrected herself, *they* didn't have love, *she* had love. Oh, God. She was a fool. Ryan had a healthy lust and affection for her, but his heart still belonged to the dead wife whom she could never replace.

And that was the problem. She wanted to give herself to him in every way there was, to show him how much she loved him with her body even if she couldn't say the words. But…she was afraid. Unbidden, the look on his face the day they'd left the hospital sneaked into her mind. Deep in her heart, she feared that Ryan would meet someone someday—someone who reminded him of Wendy and whom he could love as he'd loved his first wife.

Forcing herself to move, she resumed packing. There was absolutely nothing she could do about that. And she could hardly expect the man to forego the *normal* aspects of a marital relationship. She'd simply have to remember the circumstances under which their marriage had been arranged and protect her heart as best she could.

The sound of the opening door jolted her and she dropped the stack of socks into the suitcase in a far more haphazard manner than she usually did.

"Mission accomplished." Ryan lounged in the doorway. "The boxes are in the car. Want me to start taking down suitcases?" He indicated the ones she had closed.

She nodded. "By the time you finish, I'll have this last one ready to go."

They took the boxes home and Ryan enlisted Finn's help to carry them upstairs and unpack everything. Then he left for his office, telling her he had a few pressing things he needed to check. The trip had worn her out, and Jessie was happy to rest as Finn arranged her garments in the great big closet.

"Hey, girlfriend," he said, holding up a straight black cocktail dress. "Dynamite. I bet you look hot in this."

She grinned. "I brought it because it has no waistline and I thought if we had to go to anything formal in the next few months I might still be able to wear it."

"Ha." Finn eyed the small mound of her belly beneath the covers. "At the rate you're growing, you aren't going to be wearing anything but tents in a couple of months."

"Thanks loads. You're such a comfort."

"My pleasure."

She and Ryan's manservant, if that's what one called Finn, had reached an easy accord that delighted her. On the days she was home all day he'd begun showing her around the house, getting her acquainted slowly with the sizable rooms and their contents. He played games with her, cards and board games, which she let him win just enough to keep him happy, and they'd taken to watching one of the more ridiculous talk shows over the noon hour and commenting on the guests' dramatic problems.

He was a bit like a mother hen, fussing her to rest, fixing special meals and generally coddling her until she had to tell him to relax. She adored him.

"Finn?" she said.

"Hmm?" He was folding sweaters and zipping them into acrylic bags.

"Do you like children?"

He came out of the closet and sat on the edge of the bed. "I think so. I've never really been around them very much. I was an only child."

"So was I. What I know about babies would fit on the head of a pin."

He grinned, his boyish face lighting up. "Hope you learn fast."

"Me, too." She hesitated. "Are you going to stay when there are two little terrors ripping through this place breaking vases and tracking in muddy footprints?"

He looked at her. "You're serious, aren't you?"

She nodded. "Ryan depends on you. And so do I. I won't begin to have time to run a household of this size with two children and my gallery."

"I'm not going anywhere." Finn's slender fingers lightly brushed over the soft cashmere of the sweater he still held. "Ryan's wonderful. He's kind and…tolerant. He gave me a chance when I desperately needed one and I'll never forget that." He looked at her, his eyes sober. "I have a high school education. My partner was ten years older, well-off, sophisticated…I never needed to work. Then he got sick, and when he died, I was lost. No skills, no one to care for…when my aunt told me Ryan was willing to give me a try as a housekeeper, I was grateful even for the short-term offer.''

"He—*we*," she said, "would be lost without *you*." She gathered her courage in both hands. "I guess you must miss Wendy in your own way, as much as he does."

Finn was stroking over the sweater again, his eyes downcast, and she couldn't read his thoughts. "Wendy was so sweet," he said. "It was a terrible, terrible thing when she…passed."

"I knew her, too." She couldn't resist probing the edges of her jealousy like a child with a loose tooth. "She seemed so perfect for Ryan."

Finn's head came up. "I didn't realize you knew her. Ryan has told me that you two were childhood friends but I didn't know…" His eyes filled with tears and he reached unashamedly for a tissue on the bedside table. "Sorry. She and I were very close."

"I'm sure." Jessie waited for him to collect himself. *It's no one's fault but your own, if you feel like you're running second-best,* she told herself angrily, *even with the household help. You're the one who started this stupid conversation.*

"You look tired." Finn stood up, his gaze searching her face. "I can finish hanging these things later. Why don't you take a little nappy-poo?"

His over-the-top phrasing made her smile as she suspected he'd intended. "Good idea. I believe I will."

But after he'd left the room, it was a long time before she fell asleep.

Ryan didn't touch her again—except for a few casual kisses on her forehead—for a long time. She went to her twelve-week checkup and the doctor announced they would begin tapering her off the medication. But to her chagrin, by the time they'd decreased the dosage to half, the nausea had returned. At fourteen weeks, the doctor upped the dosage again.

She had a second sonogram then, too. This time the babies were recognizably human, with tiny ears and features.

"That's not all we can see," the technician said. "Do you want to know what you're having?"

Jessie looked at Ryan. They already knew both would be the same sex. "What do you think?"

He was grinning. "I don't know if I can stand *not* to know, now that I know *she* knows." He indicated the technician, who was laughing. "What do you think?" he said to Jessie.

"I don't know," she wailed. "On one hand, I'd like to be surprised. On the other, we have to buy so much stuff for two babies that it would be nice to know what colors to go for. All right." She took a deep breath and said to the technician, "Tell us!"

Ryan reached for her hand and threaded her fingers through his, a different clasp than the loose hold he usually employed.

The technician smiled. "You're having girls," she said. "Think pink."

"Girls." Jessie envisioned two dainty little creatures in tulle. "Ballet. Braided hair."

"Softball and soccer," Ryan countered. "Don't be sexist." He leaned over the table and set his lips gently on hers. "Congratulations, Mama."

She returned the sweet kiss, wondering if he could feel how much she loved him. "Same to you, Daddy."

They didn't go straight home. Ryan took her shopping. "Just a short trip," he said. "Then you can go home and rest."

"I don't need to rest," she said. "Other than the fact that my body can't seem to stop feeling sick, I'm fine. Whoever figured out that lethargy goes away in the second trimester was absolutely right!"

They went straight to the infant department.

One day several weeks ago, Ryan had had a special delivery made: an enormous double stroller, two high chairs, two booster seats, two baby bathtub seats and two of several other vital items the modern world deemed necessary for rearing a baby.

But today he didn't stop to look at any equipment. Instead, he took her straight to the clothing section. "Pick out some things you like," he said. "Pink, frilly, lacy, whatever. I'm going to look for some of those teeny-tiny baseball outfits I've seen."

He came back a few minutes later, bearing not outfits, but instead, two of the tiniest Red Sox baseball caps she'd ever seen. She'd chosen several sleepers and two identical dresses, not exceptionally frilly because she couldn't stand fussy clothing. And they weren't even technically pink, but a soft shade of peach.

As they were making the purchases at the register, the clerk exclaimed over the twin clothing.

"We just found out today we're having girls," Jessie told her.

"Girls." The lady sighed happily. "I have three girls. What a delight." She efficiently folded the clothing and bagged it piece by piece. "Have you talked about names?"

"Not yet." She looked at Ryan. "We haven't even begun to toss around choices."

"You'd better get started," the clerk advised. "With my first, my husband changed his mind about the name a week before my due date. When the baby was born that night, we were still arguing about it in the delivery room!''

Jessie laughed. ''I hope we won't have that problem.''

That evening Ryan's voice over the intercom informed her that they'd be eating in the dining room.

She raised her eyebrows as she got up from the nap she'd taken, washed her face and put on one of the few blouses she owned that hung out over her unbuttoned pants. They'd eaten in her room at first, and later in the kitchen when she'd been well enough to be on her feet again. The dining room was a first.

Ryan was waiting at the foot of the steps when she came down. He smiled and offered her his arm. ''Very pretty,'' he said. ''I suppose soon you're going to need a whole new wardrobe.''

''Tents, according to Finn,'' she said.

He chuckled.

''You look nice, too.'' He was wearing a sky-blue sweater that made his eyes equally vivid, and brushed wool slacks in a camel color.

''I thought we should celebrate,'' he said. ''Hearing that we're having girls today made it more real somehow.''

''I know.''

In the dining room Finn had lit candles and closed the drapes. A low fire dozed in the gas fireplace, and silver gleamed on the table. The main course was an excellent broiled salmon steak served with couscous.

''I feel so decadent, having my meals served like this,'' she confessed as they dined.

He laughed. ''I've gotten over it.'' Then he sobered. ''Do you like to cook? If you'd rather do some of your own cooking, I can ask Finn—''

''Heavens, no!'' She grinned. ''Trust me, you do not

want me cooking for you. Why do you think I ate most of my meals out when I lived alone?''

''Ah. In that case, we'll leave the current arrangements as they are. Finn genuinely enjoys it. If he doesn't, he's a darn good liar.''

''I think he's as excited about the babies as we are.''

''Speaking of our babies…'' Ryan stood and walked to the sideboard, where he picked up a dusty-looking old book and brought it back to the table. He moved her empty plate and set it before her. ''When I was bringing in those boxes from your basement, the bottom fell out of one. As I was putting things back again, this caught my eye.''

She looked carefully at the book before it. It was a Bible, clearly quite old. She ran a finger across the cover. ''Have you looked at this?''

He nodded. ''Sorry. Simple curiosity. But I found something I think you'll agree is very interesting.''

Slowly, she opened the cover of the black Bible. It was a King James version. Inside, in an elegant penmanship she didn't recognize, was her grandmother's name before she had married Brendan Reilly. ''Was this my grandmother's?''

Ryan nodded. He turned a second page and she read the inscription in the same script.

''To Ellen Kathleen Sheehan on the occasion of her First Communion.'' She glanced at him. ''I wonder if this is my great-grandmother's writing.'' Conflicting feelings warred within her. Her memories of her grandmother were tinged with fear, respect, resentment…all tied too closely to untangle. Her grandmother's voice had been sharp, often exasperated, laced with disapproval whether she had been speaking to Jessie or to her daughter, Jessie's mother. If Ellen Sheehan Reilly had ever known a moment's affection for her bastard granddaughter, as she'd once called Jessie in a fit of cold anger, it had been buried deep. Deep enough that Jessie had never felt it. Her own children were never going to wonder why they weren't lovable. They were never going to be called bastards. They were never going to pray that their best would make their mother smile just this one time.

"You know," she said, running her finger over her grandmother's name. "I think she really hated me."

"Jessie, I—"

"No, Ryan, I really think she did. You were raised with so much love you can't imagine what it was like to share a home with that woman. She was a very strong personality. My mother and my grandfather both were quiet shadows. I can barely remember my own mother. Isn't that sad?"

Ryan picked up his chair and set it down close to her, then reached for her free hand. "I'm sorry."

She nodded. "So am I. Not just for myself, but for my grandmother. Wouldn't it have been easier just to forgive my mother? To be glad that she had a healthy grandchild?"

"Yes." His voice was certain. "It would have been. I wish I could change the past for you, Jess."

She smiled sadly at him. "So do I." With an effort she forced herself to set aside the bad memories. "Was this what you wanted to show me?"

"Not exactly." He pulled the Bible to him and leafed through it to the center section where there were pages for family genealogy—births, deaths and weddings. "Look at this."

What he'd found stunned her. There were at least three generations of her family prior to her mother's birth, all neatly chronicled in the order the events had occurred.

Names leaped out at her as she scanned the pages. Corcoran, O'Driscoll, Scally. Her own name and her mother's. Her grandmother's mother had been born in Ireland, her children in Boston. Family history, even this dry and long-dead, was something she'd always assumed she'd never have.

She blinked back tears. Then she realized he was still pointing to one specific part of the page. Carefully she read the words to herself. Ellen Kathleen Sheehan. b. 9/9/18, Boston. The date of death was blank, as was her mother's, and Jessie realized no one had been left to enter those, until now. She read the next line. Shannon Mary Sheehan. b. 9/9/18, Boston. d. 9/27/18, Boston.

Goose bumps rose. She raised shocked eyes to Ryan's. "My grandmother was a twin."

He nodded, unsmiling. "And it was another girl. Any bets they were identical?"

She sat back in her chair and reached for her water glass. "I can't believe it." She reread the entry. "Poor baby. She only lived nine days." Then she sat up straight as something else occurred to her. "Did you read *all* the other entries?"

He shook his head. "No. When I saw this, I was floored. I put the book down and walked in circles for a while." He smiled crookedly. "Someday we'll have to warn our own daughters about the twin births in their family history."

Jessie reached for the Bible again, pulling it closer and carefully reading each of the entries in the flowing, slanted handwriting. "Let's look at the other generations and see— Oh!" She stopped. "There's another set born to my great-grandmother's sister. I can't believe I never knew this." The anger within her swelled. "How could they have never shared this with me?"

"Your mother may never have known," Ryan pointed out.

"That's possible," she conceded. "Probable, in fact." She shoved the Bible away from her and blew out a breath of frustration, resting her head in her hands with her elbows on the table. "Knowing twins ran in my family might have changed a lot of things,' she said wearily.

"Like what?" Ryan stepped behind her and she felt his big hands come heavily down on her shoulders. His thumbs dug in, massaging taut muscles in her neck as he rubbed her shoulders, and she let herself relax beneath his ministrations. "I wouldn't change one single thing. In a few more months you and I are going to have two beautiful baby girls." He paused, and a note of grim humor entered his voice. "I guess it's a safe bet that we won't be naming one after your grandmother."

She snorted, unamused. "Definitely a safe bet." She rolled her head, giving him better access to the bands of tension in her neck.

The room was silent for a few moments as he continued his gentle massage. Slowly his touches became less clinical and more caressing. He slid his hands partway down her arms and back up, then into her hair.

She made a sound like a satisfied cat, somewhat startled to hear it come from her own throat. Her pulse began to beat a quick tattoo. Taking a deep breath to still her nerves, she reached up and took one of his hands, drawing it forward and pressing a kiss into his palm. "That felt wonderful," she said.

He moved to her side. Slowly, looking into her eyes, he took her elbow and helped her to her feet, then put his hands at her waist as she turned to face him. "Jess," he said, and his voice was rough velvet.

She lifted her arms to circle his neck as he slipped his hands around her and drew her close, searching out her mouth, claiming her with a sure, deep possession that shook her to her toes. She opened her mouth to him, her tongue dancing a swirling sensual pattern with his as he pulled her up against his chest, flattening her breasts against the firm, hard musculature. His thighs were hard. She made another sound deep in her throat as his thick arousal found the notch at her thighs and pressed heavily forward.

How long had she needed him without even knowing it? she wondered. Love flowed through her, tightening her arms around him as she gave herself more completely to his caresses. Her pregnancy was forgotten, the doctor's warnings unheeded as she moved her hips sinuously against his, excitement spiraling high as his body responded to her provocative motions and his hands slid down her back to palm her buttocks and pull her up tight against him.

She whimpered, squirming against him, trying to get even closer. And then he tore his mouth from hers. "Stop," he panted, his voice a fierce growl. "Do—not—move."

She stopped, too dazed to comprehend.

Ryan was breathing like a bellows, harsh gasps that moved her on his chest and sent sensation sizzling clear down to her toes. Reluctantly his arms loosened and he let her slide back to the floor. He groaned as her body slid over his and she caught her breath as his hips thrust one last time. Loosening his embrace, he took her by the arms and moved her a step away from him.

"Jess," he said.

She raised her gaze to his, her bewilderment plain. "Why not?"

He smiled, though there was a distinctly pained quality to it. "Believe me, it wasn't my first choice." His hands caressed her shoulders, his thumbs sliding along her collarbones with a light, sweet touch. "There's nothing I want more than to make love to you, but we can't. Doctor's orders, remember?"

Abruptly, she *did* remember, and her whole body sagged. "Dear Lord," she said. "What was I thinking?"

His smile widened to a wolfish grin, and his eyes glittered. "You weren't. And neither was I." Releasing her shoulders, he took her left hand, raising it between them to inspect the rings that were the symbol of his claim on her. "The day the doctor gives you a clean bill of health can't come soon enough for me. But the last thing in the world that I want to do is endanger our babies."

She nodded. Her knees were still shaking from the violence of the passion that had flared between them, but she knew he was right. And she agreed. Finally she heaved a sigh, offering him a wry grin. "You're right. I don't like it, but you're right." Then she stepped forward and raised herself on her tiptoes, pressing a gentle kiss against his stubbled jaw. "Thank you for stopping." Her voice was low. "I'm not sure I would have…thought to stop."

He groaned, taking her face between his big hands and taking her mouth in one last hard kiss before releasing her completely. "Great. Thanks for sharing *that.* I'm going to have enough trouble sleeping without knowing that if I'd kept my big mouth shut—"

She put a hand over his mouth, laughing. "But what a noble gesture. You're quite the romantic—" She stopped as his face changed. How stupid had that been? She should be the first one to remember that there had been nothing remotely romantic in their marriage agreement.

Ryan cleared his throat. "You'd better go to bed now. You've been on your feet enough today."

"Yes." She couldn't wait to escape before she gave in to the tears that were pushing behind her eyes. "I think I will."

Seven

In early May. Jessie and Ryan went on an introductory tour of the hospital for expectant parents. The tours were arranged by due date, with women who'd signed up for childbirth classes near the same time in the same tour groups.

She was the only woman in their group whose belly already led the way, and she decided it was time to acquire some maternity clothing. Ryan insisted on going along. They purchased a new wardrobe of items that were made for women who were going to wind up with roughly the same dimensions as a water buffalo.

On the way home they drove past her old apartment. She'd sublet it the month before to a young urban professional type who looked as if she would take good care of it.

They headed southwest to Brookline and home. Home. It *was* home, she realized, in a way no other residence in which she'd ever lived had been. Even her condo, which she'd made hers with art and other decor, had been just a place to live, not a place she'd ever felt attached to. At the Brookline house her whole body relaxed the moment she stepped through the door, and a sense of cozy rightness enveloped her.

Growing up, she'd never quite felt like she belonged in her grandparents' home. She'd felt tolerated. With a new flash of insight, she suspected that her mother probably had felt that way, as well. She'd give a lot to know what her mother's life had been like as a young woman, before the indiscretion that had been held against her for the rest of her parents' lives. She doubted it had been much different. She couldn't imagine her grandmother as anything other than stiff and unyielding, her grandfather quietly rigid and unaffectionate. Both of them had died during her high school years, but she'd been able to manage nothing more than a dry regret that their lives hadn't been happier.

Her mother hadn't changed appreciably after they were gone. She'd been beaten down too many times to recover, Jessie supposed. Or maybe she'd lacked the maternal instinct that even now stirred so strongly in her own breast. Jessie could hardly wait for the day when she'd hold her own babies. In any case, her mother's death during Jessie's senior year in college had been unexpected but not a life-changing trauma. Deep down Jessie had been alone for a long, long time.

Now you'll never be alone again.

The thought was quite a shock. But it was true! She was going to be a mother, a *good* mother. Her children weren't simply going to tolerate her, nor she them. And she had Ryan, as well. Even though he didn't love her, even if he didn't want to stay married to her, as she feared he wouldn't once the excitement of sharing parenthood wore off, she hoped they'd stay close, in more than a physical way.

Knowing that he was attracted to her was a sweet joy, one she could hardly wait to explore. But it wasn't enough. She longed for his love, even though she knew that was a hopeless dream.

And she was very, very good at not letting herself dream. Life had taught her to be a realist, to work hard to achieve the goals she knew were within reach with a lot of hard work. But life also had taught her how to discern when a goal was out of reach. Ryan was definitely one of those out-of-reach goals.

But they would always share these precious children and deep inside she couldn't suppress a small flicker of hope that Ryan would come to care for her a little, for the babies' sakes, of course.

Of course.

After dinner that evening Jessie went up and got ready for bed. Although she had been feeling well, and the fatigue of early pregnancy no longer dragged at her constantly, she still was exhausted and more than ready for bed.

She was already in bed, reading a book about breast-feeding twins, when Ryan knocked on the connecting door between their rooms. They shared the bath but each of them had been scrupulously polite about keeping their respective doors into the bathroom closed and knocking before they entered to be sure it was unoccupied.

"Come on in," she said. She was sitting up with the covers to her waist—or where her waist had once been— wearing one of Ryan's enormous T-shirts, which she'd found made wonderfully comfortable nightshirts.

When he walked through the connecting door, she caught her breath involuntarily. He was wearing a T-shirt and navy gym shorts, and his long, muscular legs were bare but for a dusting of dark curly hair. The shorts were a soft, stretchy fabric that clung to his lean thighs and did little to hide the raw power of his male body. In one arm he carried several books.

"Baby names," he said. "We should get started. People at the office are beginning to ask me."

"We still have a while to decide," she said mildly, but she patted the opposite side of the bed. "It can't hurt to think about it."

"There are literally thousands of names in these things," he said, indicating the books. He came around the foot of the bed and dumped the books between them, then punched several of the extra pillows into place and settled back against the headboard.

She laughed. "Well, since we know they're girls, that helps a lot. Why don't we each write down twenty or so names that really appeal to us and then we'll cross-reference our lists."

He shot her a skeptical look. "That sounds incredibly organized. Can't we just go through them and shoot some possibilities into the ether?"

"No, we cannot." She leaned over and opened the drawer of her bedside table, withdrawing a writing pad and two pens. She tore off two sheets of paper, handed him one along with a pen, and said, "There."

Ryan made a face of disgust but obediently picked up one of the books and started reading. After a few minutes he said, "Are there any ground rules?"

"Ground rules?" She laid her book facedown on her stomach. "Such as?"

"Do you want names that rhyme?"

"Uck." She made a face. "No way."

"Names that start with the same letter? Have the same number of syllables?"

"You're making this harder than it has to be," she pronounced. "I just want two names that we both like. They don't have to have anything in common but that."

He nodded and went back to his book.

An hour later, she laid down her pen. "I have a pretty good list. How about you?"

He surveyed what he'd written. "Yeah. Let's compare. You start."

"Okay. What do you think of Margarita?"

His blue eyes widened an instant before he hooted. "Like the drink? Are you kidding? She'd never live that down."

"It's Spanish," she said huffily, "and very pretty." But she struck it off her list. She'd just been testing him anyway. "Renee, Renata, Lisette, Phoebe."

"Keep Renee and Lisette. Deep six the other two."

At the end of her list, she still had six of the names she had suggested, plus an additional three that had been on both of their lists. Ryan read his list and they added five more.

"Not bad," she said, "for the first try. At least now we can roll some of these around in our heads and see how they sound after a couple of days."

Two mornings later he had showered and was dressing for work early in the morning when he heard Jessie call his name. There was an odd quality in her voice, and adrenaline rushed through him as he tore open the door to her room. Was something wrong with her?

She looked up as he entered, and the fear subsided immediately. Her face was positively glowing. Her dark hair was ruffled from sleep and she still wore the T-shirt she'd slept in. She was sitting on the side of the bed with both hands on her stomach.

"Come here, quick!" she urged him.

He hitched up the trousers he'd already donned and sat beside her. His weight pressed the mattress down and she slid against his side, so he casually put an arm around her, delighting in the soft pliancy of her body. "What?"

"Here. Feel here." She grabbed his free hand and planted it on her stomach through the shirt.

A shiver of shock ran up his spine. He flattened his hand over the firm mound of her belly, ignoring the pulse drumming in his veins. Just then, his focus on her was distracted by a slight but distinct bumping against his palm. "They're moving!"

"Mmm-hmm." She circled his wrist as far as she could and tugged his hand slightly to one side. "I think you can feel them more over here."

He could. And for several moments, they sat motionless as the tiny beings stretched and turned. But it wasn't enough for him. Reaching for the edge of her T-shirt, he said, "May I...?"

A flush touched her cheek but she nodded and he took a deep breath, fighting the nearly irresistible desire to kiss her. He tugged the T-shirt up, exposing her swollen flesh, and laid his hand possessively on her, curving it over the smooth, warm globe where his children were safely ensconced, feeling the satiny texture shift with each small movement of a baby.

A feeling of content like nothing he'd ever known before permeated his entire being. *This* was the life he'd been meant for.

Impulsively he kissed the top of her bent head. To his surprise and pleasure, she responded with a quiet murmur

of pleasure, resting her head in the curve of his shoulder
and cuddling against him in a sweet intimacy that made
him wish for moments like it on a daily basis.

They stayed like that for a long time, feeling their babies move, until she looked up at him and said, "They
seem to be settling down now. I've been feeling movement for weeks but never anything like that!"

He couldn't resist the urge. Bending low, he reverently
kissed her warm, silky belly, caressing her with his hand
before straightening and tugging her shirt back into place.
"Sorry," he said. "But thank you for sharing that." He
had to clear his throat. "It was…a thrill."

"I know." She cleared her throat, too, and her voice
was soft but her eyes were steady as she said, "Ryan, you
can touch me anytime."

His heartbeat doubled at the look in her eyes. "No,"
he said. "I can't. Not the way I want to."

She nodded, sighed. "Right." And his heart beat even
faster at the acceptance implicit in the single syllable.
Then her hand stroked lightly up and down his forearm,
her fingers leaving a trail of fire in their wake. "But I
could…touch you, if you like."

What? He realized he'd croaked the single, shocked
syllable aloud. As her words arranged themselves in
meaningful syllables in his brain, his entire body tightened. A distinct stirring in his groin made him shift un-
comfortably.

"I said…"

"I know what you said! I just…just…ah, hell, never
mind." He raised both hands and speared them through
his thick dark hair in utter frustration.

"Ryan?" Her voice sounded surprisingly unsure. She
waited until he looked at her. "Am I wrong about this or

were you planning on consummating this marriage when it's medically allowed?''

"Jess." His voice sounded like someone was strangling him. "You know I want you. I haven't made it a secret. But we haven't even… We can't—''

She smiled gently. ''I don't mind if we do things in reverse order.''

Another lick of fire flashed through him and the stirring became a potential embarrassment. He exhaled heavily. "God, woman, sometimes I wonder if I'll ever know you.''

She laughed and stood up, taking his hands, and he let her draw him to his feet, facing her. "Oh, you will. I can definitely promise that you will.''

She was twisting everything he said, giving her words sexual overtones that he could barely resist. "I have to get to work," he said desperately.

Then she leaned into him, and as her belly pressed hard against the rigid evidence of his interest in her, she smiled. "So who's stopping you?''

"You little tease." He slipped his hands free of hers and gathered her closer, dropping his head and seeking her mouth. He tried to gentle himself, but he was so aroused and hot for her that the kiss was a wild mating of twisting, frantic tongues. He tore his mouth from hers, pressing a trail of openmouthed kisses along her jaw and down the sensitive flesh of her long, lovely neck. When he reached the neck of the shirt she wore, he caught the fabric in his teeth and tugged the overlarge neckline aside to bare one slender ivory shoulder.

"Ryan." She yanked handfuls of his T-shirt out of the way until she could run her palms up his bare back. She traced the muscles beneath his skin with shaking hands, then he felt her fingers sliding stealthily along his ribs, burrowing between them to seek out his nipples and tug tenderly until the small buds stood out for her ministrations, sending lightning jolts of arousal straight to his loins.

He groaned, dragging his mouth back up to take her lips in a deep, thrusting imitation of what he really wanted to do. She responded by sliding her hands down his belly, making the muscles contract sharply. And then, to his shock, she didn't stop, but ran one small hand deliberately down the distended fly of his jeans, caressing his swollen flesh with sweet pressure until he grabbed her wrist and held her hand away.

"Stop," he gasped.

She smiled against his lips. "Why?"

Why? He didn't have an answer for that one, his passion-fogged brain sluggish and dazed. She reached for him with her free hand, but he caught that one as well, drawing them up to press a kiss into each palm and hold them well away from his body.

"No." He realized he was panting, and he grinned despite his discomfort and the desire raging through his system that urged him to let her finish. He looked deep into her eyes, trying to make her understand. "Don't get me wrong, Jess. There's nothing I'd like more than to make love with you, but…I don't want it to be like this. I want us both there, all the way."

Her belly brushed against his body, and he swore beneath his breath. "I want a medal of honor for this, dammit."

The comment broke the tense sexual moment and she laughed, finally letting him move her a pace away. "All right." She put a hand to his cheek. "You're definitely too noble for your own good, Mr. Shaughnessy, but I appreciate the sentiment."

He kept away from her after that, knowing the limits of his own self-control, giving her chaste kisses on a daily basis but avoiding any repeat of the heated intimacy they'd shared in her bedroom.

In early June he got called to Seattle on an unavoidable business trip. It was the first time he'd left her since she'd been hospitalized, and her small, heart-shaped face looked woebegone when he told her what he was planning.

"Have you been postponing travel because of me?" she asked.

"Not exactly," he hedged. It wasn't entirely a lie. Though he'd had a few things come up, his presence wasn't essential to anything vital, and he'd sent one of his executive team in his place. "I haven't needed to be anyplace urgently."

"But you normally travel more than you have lately." It wasn't a question. She knew full well that he'd been in and out of town frequently in the past.

"I did." He took a deep breath. "But I've been thinking about changing some of that. The past few weeks were sort of a test—I sent some of my top people out in my place, and things went just fine." He put his hands on her shoulders and gently massaged. "I don't want to be a father whose work is more important than his children, so I'm going to start shifting more of the travel responsibilities to other employees. There still will be a few things I won't be able to get out of, but for the most part I'll be home."

She had a pensive look on her face, something sad and lonely lurking in her eyes. "I'll be back as soon as I can," he said. "I'm sorry I won't be here for the sixteen-week checkup."

She smiled then, though the expression he couldn't quite interpret was still buried in her green eyes. "It's all right," she said. "I'm a big girl, and Finn won't let anything happen to me. And the checkup is no big deal. There's no sonogram scheduled."

"I know." He hesitated, then took the plunge. "Miss me?"

To his shock, her face crumpled. "Yes," she whispered. She stepped forward into the arms he held out, and he hugged her tight to him, the bulge of their children sandwiched between them.

"I'll be back soon," he said, feeling helpless when he heard her sniff.

She nodded, stirring, and when he let her go, she stepped back. "Don't mind me. I'm just one big emotional wreck these days."

But he *did* mind. He hated leaving her, though he knew he couldn't tell her. And the way she'd clung warmed his heart all out of proportion to the act. Telling himself it was only that she was pregnant and feeling vulnerable didn't do a single thing to mitigate the elation that rose within him. He stepped forward, pulling her to him for a gentle kiss, then grinned at her and opened the door. "I'll be back before you know it."

But he wasn't. Ryan was gone for nine days. To Jessie it seemed like an eternity.

On the second day after his departure, she had her sixteen-week checkup. Once again the doctor eased her off the medication for nausea, and to her delight there was no recurrence of any illness in the days afterward. But there was something that she found even more exciting than that. She could hardly wait until Ryan got home.

He called her every evening at eight her time, no matter what. Although he didn't indicate that it was difficult, she knew that it was only five o'clock his time, and she suspected it could hardly be convenient.

The night after her doctor's appointment, he had a thousand questions. "How big did you measure? So that means the babies are growing normally? Are you sure you should try going off your medication without me there?"

She answered them all patiently, pleased at his interest despite the inner voice that reminded her he was only thinking of the twins' health.

She asked about his business dealings; he wanted to know about her plans to showcase some of the new merchandise she'd recently received. She told him how much savings Finn's obsessive coupon shopping had netted him this week and they laughed about it together.

Then he said, "Weren't you expecting a decision on that loan this week?"

The question sent her spirits plummeting as low as they'd been before she'd heard his voice. "Yes," she said quietly. "No go."

"Damn! What's the matter with these people?" Frustration colored his tone, cheering her in some inexplicable way. It was nice to know he cared.

"I *really* miss you," she said before she hung up. "I'll be glad when you're home again." And she did. The house seemed too big and too quiet with only Finn and her in it. Although they still played games and kept to their regular activities, she felt the void that Ryan's absence left.

And she realized that was what had been missing from her home before. She'd tried to make it her space with furnishings and special touches, but it had still felt like little more than a place to crash when she wasn't working. And the long hours she'd worked when she was single suddenly began to look suspiciously like a way to fill up her hours so she wouldn't have to go home alone.

Ryan had changed all that. He'd shown her how it felt to have family, to know that you were going home to share your day's doings with someone who cared, someone who was sincerely interested, someone whom you loved.

What was she going to do after the babies were born? She couldn't give up her gallery. It would be an incredible act of stupidity to assume that her financial security was assured. If Ryan tired of her— The notion was so painful she could hardly give it space in her mind, but she forced herself to consider it. She knew she never would willingly give him up, nor would she ever consider breaking up the family security she was determined her children would know. But the reality of her position was that Ryan held all the cards.

So back to her first concern—what to do after the twins came.

Initially she'd assumed she would continue working full-time and hire a nanny. Now the thought was unpalatable. Could she possibly continue to run the gallery as she had been, on a part-time basis?

Cautiously she turned the idea over in her head. Now that she was married and living with Ryan, she had far fewer expenses than before. She'd have to talk to Penny and see if she wanted to continue the current arrangement. She could formally give her certain managerial responsibilities. Even if she did expand, which was looking less and less likely, she could simply hire an additional salesperson.

A feeling of satisfaction spread through her at the idea. It could work, she thought.

Despite the nightly phone calls, the days dragged. She

began sleeping in Ryan's bed simply so she could feel closer to him. The doctor had agreed that she could resume working half days five times a week, so she was out of the house more, which was good.

But when she was home, she caught herself doing ridiculous things. One evening she spent two hours in the room they'd decided would be the nursery, lying on her back envisioning how to decorate it and where to place the furniture. Another night she amused herself by making lists of the furnishings in every single room of the house from memory. Then the following night she compared her lists to the real rooms, finding to her satisfaction that she'd done a pretty decent job of recalling all the *stuff* that was packed into her new home.

On the seventh night she told him, "I think I've found a name I can live with."

"And that would be?" His voice sounded far away.

"Olivia."

"Olivia." He repeated it, rolling it around on his tongue. "I like it. It was originally on my list."

"Don't be smug," she said, smiling though he couldn't see her. "All right. That's good. One out of two."

Then he said, "I've been thinking about names, too. What do you think of Elena?"

"Elena." She did what he had done. "Very pretty. Olivia and Elena...they sound nice together."

"You realize they're probably going to wind up being called Livvie and Lanie," he warned her.

"Oh. Well, let me think about *that*."

He chuckled. "I could live with those."

They spoke for a few minutes longer. When she replaced the telephone in its cradle, she was smiling. She couldn't wait for him to get home!

But her smile faded as she slipped between the crisp

sheets of his big bed. He'd given her little indication that he was suffering as much as she was from their separation. He had probably been propositioned by half a dozen thin, elegant, *un*-pregnant women in the past week.

And though she knew Ryan would never compromise his marriage vows, she couldn't stamp out the small ember of fear that someday he'd regret marrying a woman he didn't love.

Eight

Ryan let himself in the back door as quietly as possible. *It's a good thing we don't have a dog,* he thought to himself.

He was beat. He was home two days earlier than he'd originally projected, largely because he'd been such a demanding SOB that his Seattle team had worked around the clock simply to get rid of him faster, he suspected. He didn't care; all he wanted was to be home with Jessie. He'd called from the airport to tell her he was coming home but not to wait up since he would be very late.

Leaving his suit bag in the hallway, he made his way upstairs. Finn's small apartment was on the far side of the kitchen so there was little chance of waking him. But Jessie's room was much closer to his and he doubted she'd appreciate being awakened at two in the morning.

Although he wanted to. Badly.

What would he give, he wondered, as he passed her

closed door and let himself into his own room, to be able to slide into bed with her right now? Not even for sex, although God knew he wouldn't object to that when the doctor gave her the go-ahead, but simply to be able to hold her, to fall asleep with her in his arms. The thought was enough to make him break out in a cold sweat as he stripped off his clothes. He could barely see, but there was a dim glow coming from the almost-closed bathroom door—Jessie liked the bathroom warm, he'd learned, so she often left the gas fireplace on low.

Naked, he walked across the room to the bathroom, and after a cursory glance to be sure it was empty, he took a quick shower. He shivered as the warm water sluiced over his body, half-aroused at the mere thought of Jessie's proximity, wishing the water was her hands sliding delicately over him. As he dried off and knotted the towel around his waist, he glanced at the closed door that led to her bedroom. He'd half hoped she would awaken when she heard him, that maybe she would at least come to welcome him home after she'd given him a decent interval to dress.

But after a moment's hesitation he didn't see light under her door.

Disappointed, he turned out all the lights except for the fireplace and padded across his room to the big bed against the far wall. He left the towel on the floor next to the bed and pulled back the covers to get into bed—

—and nearly jumped out of his skin when a female voice purred, "It's about time."

"Jess! In the name of—you scared me." He relaxed the combative stance he'd assumed automatically. "What are you doing?"

Her voice was still low and inviting. "Waiting for you."

His body, always quick to respond when he thought of her, went wild at the sultry tone. He nearly reached for her, but instead he forced himself to bend and snag the discarded towel, wrapping it around his waist. He couldn't touch her the way he wanted to, and he knew better than to start something he might not be able to stop. "Waiting for me to do what?" As his eyes adjusted to the dark, he could see her outline beneath the covers on the near side of the bed.

"To come to bed." She rose to her knees and faced him, and his system suffered another shock when he saw what she was wearing. Or rather, wasn't wearing. Though there was no light but in the dim glow that filtered through from the fireplace in the next room, the diaphanous material of the short gown that fluttered around her was so sheer she might as well have been wearing nothing. As she melted against him, he put his arms around her to support her, then took a deep breath as her warm, ripe figure pressed into him.

"I take it you're glad to see me." She felt so good against him. His pulse went up another notch as her belly sandwiched the ridge of his arousal between them and he nearly groaned aloud.

She buried her nose in his neck and inhaled deeply. "Oh, Ryan, I missed you so much."

"I missed you, too." He could hear the strain in his voice. "Ah, Jess, it's not that I don't appreciate the welcome, but—"

"Oh, this isn't the welcome." She lifted her head and kissed his jaw. "That comes later."

His entire body went on full alert, if it were possible to get any *fuller* than he already was. "What do you mean?"

She relaxed even more against him and he fought not

to whimper. "The doctor gave me the green light," she said.

"The green light." Did she mean what he thought, hoped—hell, *prayed*—she meant?

"All the way?" he asked hoarsely. "No…restrictions?"

She shook her head. "No. He—"

Her words ended in a small shriek as he swept her into his arms, careful of the mound of his babies in her belly. His mouth cut off her words; he thrust his tongue deep into the soft, heated recess between her lips, boldly kissing her the way he wanted to love her. Gently, but with the greatest possible speed, he lay her full-length on the mattress and sprawled beside her, still kissing her.

One arm was beneath her neck, holding her close against him, the other cupped her jaw and stroked the soft skin of her throat, seeking out the wildly beating pulse there and gently stroking a finger down to her breastbone. Their tongues tangled and teased, telegraphing need and relief and warmth. Sliding his mouth along her jaw and up, he pressed tiny kisses to her cheekbone, her temple, her forehead, her eyelids. As he graced the tip of her nose with a tiny caress, he felt her lips against his chin.

"Welcome home."

He settled his mouth over hers again, resuming the deep, consuming kisses, holding his body under strict control while he pleasured her, wanting her to be ready, no, more than ready, *desperate* for him when he finally made her his.

His hand slipped lower and lower, barely brushing over feminine bounty until he cupped the full globe of one breast in his hand. Shaping and molding, he stimulated the taut tip of her breast, making a sound of approval deep in his throat. Her arms had been restlessly tracing the swell of muscle in his shoulders and back, but she slid them up into his hair, firmly tugging his head down until she could offer him one swollen, engorged nipple.

He tested her with his tongue, flicking over the rigid peak first, then laving slow circles around the wide, dark circle of her aureola for endless moments before he drew her completely into his mouth and began to suckle. Her back arched and her heels dug into the mattress as she sucked in one swift wordless breath.

The erotic abandon in her response nearly undid his good intentions. Lifting his mouth a fraction, he muttered against her, "I want you. Are you sure this is okay?"

"Positive," she panted. Her hands still curled into his hair and she arched her back with a soft, unintelligible sound as he teased her nipple with the rough rasp of his thumb. "Ryan," she moaned. "Don't make me wait too long."

It was all the encouragement he needed. His hand spread possessively over her belly, stroking the satiny flesh and wandering down over the bulge of her warm, smooth abdomen, and he caught his breath when his fingers snagged in the soft, curling thatch of hair between her legs. She moved restlessly, shoving her hips against him. He was overwhelmed by her, by the moment, by the realization that she was going to be his after all these years. He wanted to tell her he loved her as he urged her legs apart with a shaking hand, but his tongue wouldn't form the words. She'd been so skittish when he'd first suggested marriage that he knew confessing his feelings would send her running.

And as his fingers slipped into the moist, humid crevice and he found slick, waiting heat, the last thing he wanted to do was break the mood. He drew his moistened fingers back, over the pouting bud he discovered at the top of the sweet vee of her legs, and began to rub small, gentle circles. She sucked in a breath and moaned.

"Ah," he said, "do you like that?" He still had one arm beneath her head and he leaned over her, searching out her lips again before she could answer, kissing her with the same tender care he was lavishing on her body.

His own body pulsed and throbbed against her thigh, and as she shifted beneath his hands, her hip caressed him eagerly.

She moved her arms down from his neck, stroking the furred patch of skin over his breastbone. Soon, though, her hands clutched at him helplessly as he drove her higher and higher into the heights of pleasure, and short, breathless cries escaped her throat with each soft stroke of his hand. Relentlessly he drove her on and on, his own body balanced on the knife edge of control as he brought her to the brink with his hand. Her head thrashed back and forth on his arm and she sobbed, "No, no...I want to feel you..."

"What?" He slowed his pace a fraction. "What do you want?"

Her hands moved from his hair down to grip his shoulders, then slipped farther down to tug at his waist, though she couldn't budge him. "I want you...inside me," she pleaded.

In an instant he withdrew his arm from beneath her neck and rose to his haunches, draping her legs wide over his thighs as his jutting flesh kissed the damp, satiny portal of her body. He shuddered. "I don't want to hurt you."

"You won't." She lifted her arms open to him. "Now. Please?"

He shuddered again, nearly undone at the honest need in her plaintive tone. Guiding the blunt tip of his arousal into position with a shaking hand, he slowly, slowly flexed his hips, forcing her open as he invaded her soft channel. "Jess." His voice was little more than a guttural growl as he felt the dance of satisfaction skipping up his spine. "I...I can't wait."

"Then don't." As he hovered over her and began a slow, careful thrust and retreat, she moaned and wrapped her legs around his hips. The action abruptly pulled him deeper, much deeper, and suddenly the world exploded. He leaned forward, bracing himself over her on his arms, his stroke increasing as her hips slammed up to meet his. She was crying again, sharp screams of pleasure, and he could feel himself losing control. He put a hand between them and pressed firmly down just above their joining, and her eyes flared so wide he could see them even in the dark as her body began to convulse. At the same time his frantically pumping hips surged wildly forward, jetting endless streams of release deep inside her as her hidden inner muscles gripped his hard flesh. Finally, when the last sweet shocks of pleasure had passed, they both were spent and quiet, but for the gasping sounds of their breathing.

He was careful not to let his weight crush her, and after a moment to gather himself, he pulled back from the warm haven of her body and slid to her side, gathering her in his arms. Leaning over her, he took her mouth in a sweet, lingering kiss before he lay back on the pillow beside her.

It had been everything he'd known it would be with her. And if there was any small corner of his heart she hadn't already owned, she had it now as she returned the kiss with a generosity and warmth that made him wonder once again if there was hope that she could love him someday.

* * *

Her whole body throbbed from his possession. Leisurely she turned onto her side and laid her palm over his heart. Love for this man who had shared so much of her life, and now shared everything, coursed through her and she had to bite her tongue to keep from blurting out her feelings. It was difficult to remind herself that though he cared for her and certainly had enjoyed her, he still carried Wendy in his heart. So she contented herself by saying, "I'm glad you're home."

Though it was dark, she could hear the smile in his voice. "I'm glad I'm home, too."

She laughed gently. "I'll just bet."

He stirred then, gathering her closely against him so that their babies rested between them and she was wrapped in his arms. "I hated being away from you."

"I hated you being away," she responded, touched by the vehemence in his tone. "But you didn't have to worry. I'm doing well, and Finn would have called you immediately if there'd been a problem."

He turned his head, and his whiskered chin brushed her cheek as he pressed a kiss to her temple. "It wasn't the worry," he said quietly. "I missed *you,* Jess. I can't imagine my life without you now."

She was stunned. Pleasure of an entirely different kind exploded through her at his words. And hope followed in its wake, revived. Was it possible Ryan could let go of his past and learn to love her? There had been something in his voice she'd never heard before. She was afraid to even give it a name. But she snuggled closer against him as hope rushed through her once again, and when her eyes closed, her heart was lighter than it had been in a long time.

* * *

They settled into a routine after that night, and he'd never felt happier in his entire life as the next few weeks passed. Jessie worked part-time, usually going to the gallery in the afternoons. By the time he got home in the evening, she was refreshed and interested in hearing about the things in which he currently was involved. After dinner they watched television or pored over baby books and catalogues, looking for things for the nursery they were slowly putting together. And after that…after that came the part of the day he looked forward to from the time his eyes opened in the morning.

Apparently, his satisfaction with his life showed, because people remarked on it and congratulated him on his marriage everywhere he went. One day as he was leaving after a lunch in the restaurant that occupied the old Federal Reserve Bank at the Hotel Le Meridien, a man passing through the door hailed him.

It was Mort Brockhiser, a friend as well as the vice president in charge of commercial loans at Boston Savings Bank.

"Good to see you, Ryan," Mort said, shaking his hand vigorously. He was a small, rotund man with a fringe of graying hair stretching from each temple around the back of his head, and he had a habit of smoothing his hand over the shining crown of his bald head. "Emmy and I extend our congratulations on your marriage."

"Thanks, Mort." Ryan had known Mort and his wife, Emmy, since his senior year at M.I.T., when he'd applied for the patent on Securi-Lock and Mort had backed his loan request to start production of the technology. "How's your family?"

"Fine, fine. Youngest is finishing at Harvard this year. I'm going to be throwing a 'No More Tuition' party next May." He chuckled at his own wit, then went on. "Maybe you and the wife could join Emmy and me for dinner some night. Where'd you find this lady? Emmy's dying to hear all the details.''

"We grew up together," Ryan said. No point in trying to explain anything else; it sounded too crazy. "Her maiden name was Reilly. Jessie Reilly."

A sudden look of comprehension settled over Mort's face. "Of The Reilly Gallery?"

Ryan nodded. "One and the same."

"She applied for a loan a few months ago," Mort said. "I visited her shop. Very nice. Would have liked to make the loan, but you know how cautious the board is these days. Her financials were a little shaky." Then his eyes narrowed thoughtfully and he chuckled. "But I guess they're not shaky anymore."

"Jessie's very independent and an excellent saleswoman," Ryan said. "If I were you, I'd back anything she chose to try." And if he were a banker, he would. He had faith in her business acumen. And he'd become intimately acquainted with her shop and the things she stocked. She had great instincts, which was half of what it took to survive in the market.

"Hmm." Mort nodded once, then the intensity faded from his gaze. "As I said, we'll have dinner."

Ryan nodded. "Jessie would like that, but it may have to wait awhile. We're expecting twins in October."

Mort's eyes bulged. "Good Lord!" He had two sons of his own. "You're going to have your hands full."

"I know." And he loved the thought of it.

The weeks passed and so did the seasons. Spring slid into summer, and Jessie grew larger and larger as their babies grew inside her. They still were able to make love, and to his delight she was endlessly inventive and far more agile than her increasing bulk indicated. And when they lay together afterward, when she snuggled into his arms and laid her head on his chest, his heart felt as if it were going to swell and burst right out of him with the feelings he struggled to hide.

One afternoon he gave Finn the night off and came home well before Jessie was expected, to prepare a surprise for her. He'd bought roses, a stunning bouquet of red and pink ones to symbolize the love he hoped they were beginning to share, as well as the friendship they'd had for so long.

Before Finn left to visit his mother, he prepared a spinach salad and a platter of cold roast beef. Ryan had called that morning and asked him to set the glass-topped wrought-iron table for them on the terrace, and when he took the vase of roses up, he discovered Finn had done far more than simply set the table.

It was covered in a white linen cloth with snowy napkins gracing the porcelain plates. Waterford goblets for wine and water sparkled in the late-afternoon light. There were candles on the table, and two large brass candelabra with white tapers were strategically placed with an arrangement of potted palms and ferns around them. He set the vase of roses on a side table and noted the bottle of Dom chilling in the ice bucket. Good. Very good.

He took a deep breath. He'd made up his mind. Tonight he was going to do it.

Tonight, he was going to tell Jessie he loved her. That he'd loved her for what seemed like forever, that she made him happier than any man had a right to be. If he was right about the feelings growing between them, she would return the words. And his life would be complete.

Leaving the terrace, he went down to his room for a quick shower and changed into casual linen pants and a cotton shirt with a faint blue stripe. She loved him, he was nearly sure of it. If she didn't, she should be in Hollywood. She'd be a shoo-in for an Oscar.

He rummaged in his drawers for a pack of matches. The big lighter was downstairs, but he was pretty sure he'd seen matches here somewhere…they probably were in Jessie's room. Finn was always lighting good-smelling candles in there.

As he moved into her room, he thought again of the way she moved into his arms for a passionate kiss every morning before he left the house. The way she greeted him with shining eyes and another kiss in the evening. The way she moved with him when they made love, as if she knew exactly what he wanted and how to please him utterly. Last week she'd brought home a hand-blown glass paperweight in the forty shades of Ireland that she'd ordered for the store. But she'd given it to *him* because, she told him, she knew he'd like it in his office. She could have given him a piece of limestone and he'd have liked it, because she'd thought of him.

He pulled open the drawer of her bedside table. No matches.

Moving to the dresser on which sat a fat, scented candle, he opened the first drawer. Pay dirt. As he reached in for the match box he'd located, a folded piece of paper atop the dresser caught his eye.

Dining room, it was labeled in Jessie's handwriting. Slowly, he picked up the sheet of paper and unfolded it. Shock replaced incredulity as the words penetrated, and that in turn was replaced by a burgeoning pain. A leaden weight encased his heart as he read down the page:

Sideboard: Kirk-Steiff silver tea service, Kirk-Steiff cutlery for twelve, two Irish lace tablecloths, twenty-four linen dinner napkins. Breakfront: Waterford crystal goblets—champagne, water, three kinds of wine...

There were several sheets of paper. List after list of the rooms in his home and the contents of each. She'd been *casing* the place, for God's sake!

Carefully, he folded the papers exactly as they had been. He felt as if he couldn't take a deep breath as he closed the drawer and walked back through the bathroom to his room. *What an idiot you are,* he told himself bitterly. *You knew going into this that Jessie didn't marry you for love.* And now that he thought about it, he was sure his financial status had a lot to do with her decision to recruit him to father her children.

"Ryan? Where are you?"

He sucked in a deep breath. He wasn't ready to face her. Blowing it out, he met his own gaze in the mirror. No choice. "I'm up here," he called. "Bedroom."

He stayed where he was, listening as her footsteps tripped lightly up the steps and came down the hall. She entered her own room first and came through the bathroom to find him.

"Guess what?" Her voice was jubilant and her whole face was alight. She looked so beautiful and vivacious that his heart squeezed viciously into a small, tight knot.

"What?" His own voice sounded distinctly unenthusiastic to his own ears but she didn't appear to notice.

"I got a loan! The Reilly Gallery is officially going to expand." She came straight to him and threw her arms around his neck. "Oh, Ryan, I'm so happy!"

Automatically he put his hands at the sides of where her waist used to be. "That's great." He worked hard to make his voice sound more normal. Carefully he set her away from him and walked into the bathroom, going to the faucet and washing his hands to give himself something to do. "When do you plan to start?"

"Right away." She followed him, still smiling, but when he glanced at her there was a puzzled, wary look in her eyes. "I've already spoken to the owner of my building about leasing that empty space next to the gallery and knocking down a wall. He didn't seem to think there would be any problem."

"No grass growing under your feet." He forced himself to turn and smile at her. "Hungry? You can tell me all about it over dinner."

"Starving," she said, "but we might be forced to fend for ourselves. Finn's not here, and the table isn't set in either room downstairs."

"I, uh, I asked Finn to set a table for us on the terrace," he said, seeing no way to get out of it. If she'd come home just a few minutes later... "I'll go get the food and send it up in the dumbwaiter."

"Okay. Just let me change and I'll be up."

He went down to the kitchen, glad to escape for the moment. *Idiot!* he thought again. How could he have let himself think for a minute that she cared for him? Just because they'd found a great deal of physical satisfaction together didn't necessarily mean her emotions were involved.

She was faster than he'd expected, and he barely beat her up to the terrace on the roof. Wheeling the cart loaded with food over to the table, he concentrated on setting everything in place as she approached.

"This is lovely," she exclaimed. "It looks so...so romantic." Her voice dropped.

"You know Finn. I guess he got a little carried away," he said casually. "Looks nice, but the candles are overkill.'' Briskly he grabbed the candelabras and carried them to the far side of the terrace, then dragged the potted trees back to their original positions spaced around the fringes of the furniture. There was nothing he could do about the flowers or the wine, he supposed. He'd just have to live with those.

Jessie's face, when he dared to glance her way, wore a slightly disturbed expression. Probably relief. When she'd seen the romantic setting, he imagined she'd feared he was going to do something stupid. Something like telling her he loved her...

Stop whining, Shaughnessy, he ordered himself. *You wanted her, you wanted babies. You got both. You never expected her to love you, anyway. Not really.*

Thank God he'd seen those notes. Ignoring the throbbing ache in his heart, he held her chair. ''Have a seat and tell me about your loan.''

Jessie hesitated. Then, casting him a glance from beneath her lashes, she slid into the chair. As he took his own seat, he casually moved the roses off to one side.

''Are you going to open the wine?'' she asked.

''Uh, I wasn't planning on it,'' he said. ''You're not supposed to be drinking. I don't know what Finn was thinking when he set that out.''

''One glass of wine would be all right.''

''I don't want to take any chances with these babies.'' He couldn't look at her. ''We'll save the real celebration for when your store's completed.''

''Is something wrong?'' Her voice sounded uncertain.

''Not at all.'' He forced himself to meet her troubled gaze. ''So talk to me.''

''All right.'' She continued to watch him. ''Let's see...what do you want to know?''

''Who made you the loan?''

"Boston Savings. Can you believe it? They were polite but absolutely adamant when I made my pitch before."

Boston Savings. It couldn't be a coincidence that he'd seen Mort Brockhiser and now she'd gotten a loan from Brockhiser's bank. "Did he say what changed?" he asked neutrally.

"No. I asked him that, too. He said he'd thought all along I was a good prospect and that he was glad the board of directors had a change of heart." Her smile flashed in the evening light. "I'm too happy to care *what* was said, as long as they make me that loan!"

That was good. He decided not to tell her about his conversation with Mort. It wasn't as if he'd cosigned her note or anything like that. And, anyway, hadn't she married him for the financial benefits that came with him?

Nine

Ryan was behaving strangely.

He shooed her off to get ready for bed after dinner, telling her he would take care of the dishes. In the past they'd cleaned up together on the infrequent nights when Finn wasn't around. Jessie couldn't shake the feeling that he wanted to get rid of her, and the idea hurt her feelings. She thought they'd broken through a barrier to a new level of intimacy when they'd begun making love. Tonight Ryan was acting as if he didn't really want her around.

And what the heck was the deal with that dinner? When she'd walked out onto the terrace, her heart had leaped into her throat. The greenery and candelabra made a stunning backdrop for the roses, and the table service had gleamed in the evening sun. It had made a lovely, romantic picture, and she still wondered if Ryan hadn't asked Finn to set it up and then changed his mind for some unknown reason.

It was depressing.

She caught sight of herself in the mirror and sighed. Speaking of depressing—it was the beginning of July and she still had more than a third of this pregnancy to go. Already she looked like she'd swallowed helium balloons. How long would Ryan continue to be attracted to someone he couldn't even get his arms around?

She shucked off the oversize denim blouse and navy shorts with the stretchy front panel, then tossed them into the clothes basket along with her underwear. Donning a short silk robe, she headed into the bathroom and prepared for bed. Then she climbed into ''her'' side of the large bed she'd shared with Ryan for the past few weeks.

She was reading a book on infant growth when Ryan came into the room, and she set it down with a stifled yawn. "I'm glad you came up. I'm getting sleepy."

He didn't respond, though he smiled absently at her. Emptying his pockets, he stripped to his briefs and got ready for bed, then removed those and got under the covers on his side of the bed. When he turned out his light, she did the same.

She waited for him to reach for her and draw her into his arms, but tonight he merely laid one hand over the swell of her belly. "Lots of movement today?"

"Tons. But they're pretty quiet right now." She placed her hand over his. "Did something happen at the office today that upset you?"

He was silent for a long moment. "No," he said finally. "What makes you think that?"

"I don't know. You just seem…subdued." *Withdrawn.*

In the darkness she felt him shrug. "It was just one of those days, I guess." His hand began to trace small circles over her belly. "How are you feeling physically?"

She chuckled wryly, covering the hurt that sprang up

when she realized he was shutting her out. "Huge. I can't imagine getting much larger, but I know I will." She still couldn't avoid the conviction that something was wrong, but he didn't seem willing to share his problems, and she didn't know how else to let him know she wanted to be there for him. Then her attention faded from her concern as he continued to stroke her body.

The gentle circles grew larger, and his big, warm hand brushed over her breast. She sucked in a sharp breath of pleasure as sensation cut a jagged path through her. Her breasts were so sensitive right now that even his lightest touch brought heat flowing to her abdomen and made her pulse race. "Your skin is so soft," he breathed, "so smooth. I love touching you."

"I love it when you touch me, too." She shifted toward him for a kiss, resisting the impulse to blurt out *I love you*.

But he wouldn't let her turn to him. Instead, he rolled her onto her side and snuggled behind her, drawing her into the heat of his large body and cradling her head on his arm. He drew his knees up, and the rough hair along his legs brushed the backs of her thighs. The movements of his awakening flesh pressed against the soft flesh of her buttocks, and he flattened his palm against her abdomen. She squirmed as the pressure of her tightly closed legs created an erotic pleasure, then she gasped as his fingers slipped beneath her top leg and drew it up over his.

The motion pressed him forward, his hips firmly pushing at the tender cleft between her legs, and she moaned. His big hand slid up over her, cupping and stroking her breasts, his rough thumb rasping over the tender nipples until she was moving desperately against him, her pulse hammering in her throat and at the apex of her thighs. He lifted his head and caught her earlobe between his teeth, lightly scoring the tender flesh and then soothing the small sting with his tongue. He pressed a string of kisses down her neck and along the smooth plane of her shoulder. At the same time, he slipped his hand down over the mound of her belly to the hidden cove beneath, combing his fingers through the moist curls he found there.

When he lightly pressed down with one finger, she cried out at the waves of intense pleasure that burst through her, then buried her face in the pillow as one long finger slid stealthily into her humid channel. Her hips bucked and writhed, and he groaned softly into her ear, then lightly nipped at her shoulder.

She swept her hand back and down between their straining bodies, finding and freeing his swollen shaft, drawing him forward to the portal of her feminine flesh, wordlessly urging him to complete their union. Ryan spread his palm over her abdomen again, holding her in place, and she felt the blunt probe of the broad head slowing pushing into her, filling her.

He began to move, a slow steady retreat and advance, repeating the motion until she turned her face from the pillow and hissed, "Move!"

He laughed then, deep in his throat. "Take it easy. What's your rush?"

Reaching back her hand, she smacked him smartly on the buttocks, and he laughed again, capturing her hand and crossing it over her chest so he could shackle her wrist with his other hand. Then he replaced his hand on her abdomen, sliding his middle finger relentlessly down to trace small circles on the throbbing nub of her desire. She could feel her climax approaching, roaring down upon her to crash over her head, drowning her in spiraling ripples of sensation as her inner muscles clenched around his engorged flesh. Behind her his steely body grew taut as his own release ripped through him. He pushed himself hard against her, emptying himself in shaking, groaning pulses as she shivered and quaked around him.

Their bodies were slick with sweat as their heartbeats slowed, and after a moment Ryan reached down and tugged the tangled sheets into place without moving himself from her. He kissed her neck, but when she turned her face up to his, he merely nuzzled her temple and said, "Go to sleep, cupcake."

And as she snuggled into his arms and her eyelids drifted shut, she was disturbed. Though the distance he'd seemed to want between them earlier had vanished in the fire of their passion, she sensed something had shifted in his feelings for her.

And she was fairly sure the shift wasn't a good one.

At twenty-four weeks, a third sonogram confirmed the twins' continued health. In August her twenty-eight week check-up passed and by the beginning of September Jessie was nearly thirty-two weeks pregnant.

"I go to the doctor again tomorrow," she reminded Ryan the evening before her next appointment. Things had been good between them since the night of that weird "dinner that wasn't," although she often felt a little frustrated by his seeming determination to keep her at an emotional distance. Physically he was as passionate as he'd been since the first night they'd made love, but she sensed something…something she couldn't put her finger on, although she was sure it wasn't simply her imagination working overtime.

"I know." He smiled at her over the top of the *Wall Street Journal* he was reading. "I have it on my office calendar. I'll come home in time to drive you." He folded the paper and laid it down. "This weekend we need to get the nursery finished. I know things seem to be going really well, but if you deliver early, we have to be prepared."

"If I deliver too early," she said seriously, "they won't be coming home right away."

"Think positive." He rose and came over to the chair where she'd been sitting, reading. Putting his hands beneath her elbows he carefully helped her to her feet, then drew her into his arms, but he didn't seek out her lips as he once would have done. At the same time his big hands massaged her back, finding all the tender spots that were giving her trouble as she carried around more and more baby weight. According to the doctors, the twins were a healthy size. Good for them, not so good for her. She felt like a beached whale. It was hard to get from a sitting position to a standing one, impossible to put on her socks or tie her shoes. She was exhausted after climbing the stairs, although she rarely had to, since Ryan forbade it and carried her up and down.

She relaxed in his embrace and let him take her weight. "Umm," she said against his shoulder, "I'll give you about three days to stop doing that."

Above her head, he chuckled. "I can see we've established a pattern for life here. I'm not going to get out of this after the babies are born, am I?"

"Not a chance." She rested her head on his shoulder, pleased that he was speaking of long-term issues. "I wish the next couple of weeks would hurry and pass. I'm tired of feeling fat and ugly. I'm tired of having my back hurt and my feet swell. I'm tired of feeling tired."

He was still rubbing her back with light, soothing strokes. "I know. Soon it will be over, and you'll be your old self."

"Will that make you happy?" Since the night they'd first made love, he'd seemed utterly enthralled with her body, pregnant or not. But recently little things had bothered her. She tried to tell herself it was her imagination, but there was no denying the fact that outside their bed Ryan avoided the intimacies they'd been beginning to share.

Now he shrugged. "I'll be happy for your sake, but I think you're absolutely beautiful the way you are." Putting a hand beneath her chin, he tilted her face up so that he could look deep into her eyes. "You've always been beautiful to me, Jess. There hasn't been a day since you were about thirteen that you didn't take my breath away."

She felt as if her heart were going to stop at the sincere tone of his declaration. *Was he telling her he loved her?* Or merely that she'd turned him on for years? "Why didn't you ever say anything," she asked cautiously, "back in high school?"

He made a rough sound of derision and let her go, stepping a pace away. "You were with the football player," he said quietly. "What chance would I have had?"

"I...I don't know," she said honestly. Happiness warred with a growing touch of...annoyance? No, not strong enough. Anger? Too strong. Hurt was perhaps the best word for what she was feeling. "Do you—"

"Ryan?" Finn came to the door of the den, and they both turned toward him. "Excuse me. I have some things you need to go through from when I cleaned closets yesterday. There's some stuff you might want."

"All right," Ryan said. He looked back at her, and his eyes were wary. "Do you want to look through it with me?"

She nodded, aware that an important moment had just

been lost, equally aware that there might never be another one unless she exposed her soul and took a chance that there was more between them than affection, attraction and history.

They followed Finn to the big eat-in kitchen where he had several boxes stacked near the door. "I'm going to the store," Finn said. "Just leave anything you don't want, and I'll take care of it."

A moment later, they were alone in the kitchen.

"I wonder what's in these?" Ryan said. His voice was so normal that she wondered if it bothered him at all that they hadn't finished exploring what he'd started. He ripped the tape on the top one and opened the flaps, peering into the box. "College stuff," he said. "Textbooks." He lifted it to one side and moved to the next box in the stack.

Jessie moved closer as he opened it. Then his face lit up. 'What is it?'' she asked.

He grinned at her. "Baby stuff!" he said.

"Baby stuff?" Why on earth would they have had baby things stored in a closet? She didn't remember putting anything away anywhere but the nursery.

"When we first started talking about having a family, Wendy did the nesting thing," he said. "Look through here and see if you'd like to keep anything." He lifted out a gorgeous white baby afghan crocheted in an intricate shell pattern, and there was such a tender expression on his face that she mentally cringed. "I remember when she made this. Won't Olivia or Elena look nice all bundled up in this?"

"Umm." She made a noncommittal sound, trying desperately to keep the hurt and humiliation from showing. "I, ah, just remembered something I have to tell Penny. I'll use the phone in the study."

He looked at her then, eyebrows raised. "You can use the one in here."

"No, I, ah, that's okay." She turned and fled, as fast as it was possible for a two-ton tank to flee. When she got to the study, she ducked inside and closed the door, leaning heavily against it.

Hot tears streaked down her cheeks like trails of fire. She took one trembling breath, then another. That he could so casually rave about Wendy only moments after she thought they'd been on the verge of a momentous discussion told her more clearly than any words what her role in Ryan's life was. And it wasn't that of a dearly loved wife.

She was still brooding the next day at the store when she got a telephone call from her landlord, wanting to know if she intended to lease her condo again. If she didn't, he continued, the woman to whom she'd sublet it wanted to stay there with a lease of her own.

Pleading business, she put him off to give herself time to think about it. Her first impulse had been to tell him she did want to renew the lease. She didn't need to, now that she was married and living with Ryan, but...when she confronted the little voice in her head that urged her to keep her lease, she realized why she was hesitating about letting it go.

As long as Ryan still held Wendy in his heart, their future together would always be uncertain. True, they would share children, which she was more and more certain he regarded as something that would bond them for life. The question was, could she share him with a memory? She was far less certain of that.

And then there was her other fear, one far more real than the ghost of his ex-wife. Ryan's face on the day they'd seen the nurse who resembled Wendy had burned a permanent scar in her heart. What if he found another woman like Wendy someday? Wendy had been as different from Jessie as day was from night. If he'd been drawn to a woman like Wendy once, might not there be a chance he'd be drawn to another one someday? His convictions about marriage and family might be sorely tested if he ever fell in love again. And if that happened, where did that leave her?

High and dry. Alone. As she'd been most of her life.

And because her innate caution urged her not to do anything rash, she called her landlord back and arranged a time to sign the new contract right before her appointment at the bank to sign the loan papers.

As she made her way into the bank after meeting her landlord, she was conscious of a ridiculous sense of… relief? Not exactly the correct word. But she knew she'd been right to keep her lease in place, if only because having the condo made her feel more secure, as if she still held the reins of her future.

"Mrs. Shaughnessy! Thank you for coming." Mr. Brockhiser, her loan officer, walked across the lobby as he extended a hand.

"It's my pleasure, believe me." She smiled at the man as they shook. "I was delighted to get your call. Enlarging my gallery is something to which I'm totally committed."

Brockhiser showed her into his office, then took a seat behind his desk. His eyes twinkled as he shuffled papers. "That's good, but you're certainly going to have your hands full once those babies arrive, aren't you?"

"Yes, but I—" She stopped. "How did you know I'm having more than one baby?"

"Ryan told me." The banker winked at her. "Understand you two were childhood sweethearts. My wife's dying to meet you."

"Um, we grew up together, yes." She cleared her throat. "I didn't realize you knew Ryan."

Brockhiser folded his hands atop the stack of papers. "Oh, we go way back. I knew him before he was a big success. That man has the magic touch. When he said he'd back anything you chose to do, I figured I'd go back to the loan committee with your request. You should have told me you were married to Ryan—I'd have been able to make you the loan right off the bat."

Jessie froze as the room seemed to recede, leaving her in an airless vacuum of shock. *So that's why I got the loan. Ryan guaranteed it.*

The moment was engraved in her mind with stark clarity—the banker's beaming face, the sunlight slanting across the office, the rough, tweedy fabric of the chair in which she sat. Carefully, trying to keep her voice level, she said, "Could you excuse me for a moment, Mr. Brockhiser?" She was out of the chair before he could assist her, waddling across the lobby and around the corner to the ladies' room she'd located in the bank on an earlier visit.

Behind her the banker's concerned voice asked, "Are you ill, Mrs. Shaughnessy?" But she didn't stop.

God was merciful and the ladies' room was empty. Pausing for a bare second to lock the door behind her, she sank onto the settee in the lounge area, taking deep breaths to suppress the heaving sobs that strove to burst forth.

God, she couldn't believe it. He knew, he *knew* she'd wanted to do this without his assistance. How could he have gone behind her back like that? A few tears leaked out, and as she blotted them she told herself they were tears of anger.

But deep in her heart she knew better. Ryan had given

her hope for a future she'd never dared to believe in before.

She hadn't let herself dream of love, of a lifelong marriage, because she knew it would destroy her if she let down all the carefully built walls of bitter experience. She hadn't seen that kind of love in her own life, and she was afraid—no, *terrified*—to even allow herself to think for one single second that it might exist. But Ryan had slowly excavated beneath the foundations of that fear, and even though she knew she could never be everything he longed for in a wife, she'd begun to hope that she could give him enough to last them a lifetime. She'd offered him children, her unspoken devotion, a warm happy marriage based on friendship and passion—and he'd thrown it back in her face.

He knew how she felt about accepting money from him, knew how important it was to her to be independent. And he'd ignored her feelings completely. If he loved her he'd have taken her feelings into consideration.

And that was the bottom line. She'd been kidding herself, deluding herself into imagining that they could build a life together. But they couldn't. Not *together*.

Because Ryan wasn't interested in *together*.

Ryan slammed down the phone in a rare display of temper.

Where was she? He'd called the gallery three times that morning, and Penny had told him each time that Jessie was out of the building and she didn't know where she was or when she'd return.

He'd initially called simply to invite her to have lunch with him, but when he'd realized she was out of touch, his anxiety level had rapidly grown to mammoth proportions. What was she thinking? A woman in her condition, especially with the added risk of carrying twins, should never just wander off without telling anybody where she was going.

Three weeks had passed since the day she'd walked out of the kitchen with that odd look on her face, and though he knew the moment had been a defining one in their relationship, he still hadn't figured out exactly what in hell it had defined.

She'd slept in her own room that night, pleading an upset stomach, and he hadn't had any opportunity to talk to her. The next day she'd gone for her thirty-two-week checkup, and as if the doctor were in cahoots with Jess, he'd prohibited any sexual activities until after the babies were born. She hadn't come back to his bed since. And though he'd attempted to tease her into it, she'd merely replied seriously that she wasn't sleeping well because of her bulk and the babies' movements and that she'd keep him awake. And the few times Ryan had tried to bring up that day in subtle ways, she'd managed to avoid talking about it—or even looking him straight in the eye, for that matter.

What the hell had gone wrong? Could she be upset by those baby things he'd discovered? Could she possibly be bothered by the reminders of his life with Wendy? He could hardly imagine Jess minding that. She'd loved Wendy, too. And besides, he was sure it was painfully evident that he'd never had feelings for Wendy like the all-consuming emotions that Jess roused in him. No, any suspicion that she might be jealous was only a product of his own desperate imagination.

Still, he'd tactfully put everything back in the box and set it in the closet of the nursery—only to find a few days later that Jessie had unpacked the box. The white afghan Wendy had made was draped over the back of a rocking chair, the small sweater set with its matching hat hung in the closet. So obviously he'd been off base.

His office phone rang and he realized it was his private line. Snatching up the receiver, he barked, "Yes?"

"Ryan?"

It wasn't Jessie, and his whole body sagged in disappointment. "Speaking."

"It's Mort Brockhiser. I think your wife might be ill."

It took him a moment to put the pieces together. Finally he asked, "She's at the bank?"

"Not anymore." The lender's voice conveyed his concern. "She came in to sign her loan papers, but a minute after we sat down she bolted for the ladies' room. I waited but she never came back and one of the tellers just told me he saw her leaving the bank a moment ago."

Dear Lord, let her be all right. Aloud, he said, "Thanks for calling, Mort. I'd better go home."

He called the house from his car phone but she wasn't there yet and her cell phone shifted him to voice mail so she must have it turned off at the moment. Finn promised to call him the moment she showed up. She wasn't at the shop, either, and Penny still hadn't heard from her, though she also promised to call him, concern clear in her voice.

But by the time he pulled into the garage, his car phone still hadn't rung. Finn met him at the door. The manservant was practically wringing his hands with worry. "Where could she be?" he asked.

"I don't know." He punched in the admissions department at the hospital where they'd done preadmission work, but she hadn't been admitted. Nor had the doctor's office heard from her.

Panic was an ever-present companion beating wildly at the edges of his mind but he grimly refused to allow it a toehold. Without a clear idea of where he intended to go, he decided to head back downtown. If she'd been at the bank, she could be sitting in any number of little cafés or coffee shops in the area. Though why she wouldn't call if she were ill or—his all-consuming worry—in labor was a mystery.

The phone in his car rang, and he pounced on it. "Hello?"

"Ryan, she's home." It was Finn.

"Thank God." A relief so intense he felt like sliding right down onto the rubber floor mat flooded through him. "Is she all right?"

"I...I don't know. She went straight up to her room and asked not to be disturbed."

He was already making an illegal U-turn and heading back to Brookline. "I'll be there in ten minutes."

In reality it took him less than ten.

He was out of the car before the engine had completely died and took the stairs two at a time, throwing his summer jacket at Finn on the way to her room. "Jess! Where the hell *were* you? I've been worried *sick*—"

"Stop worrying. I'm fine. The babies are fine." Her voice cut through his frantic response, cool and measured, and as her tone registered, he stopped in midstride.

"Did something happen?" he asked cautiously.

"No." Again her tone was cool.

Something was wrong, very wrong, but he couldn't imagine what it could be. He studied her for a moment. She looked fine, if a little pale.

Then he realized what she was doing. Packing. There was a half-filled suitcase on the bed and she was systematically emptying each of the drawers of her dresser. "What are you doing?"

"Packing."

Frustration began to eat at the edges of his control,

fueled by the adrenaline still rushing through his system. He hadn't meant it in a literal sense. "Why?"

She shook her head, looking down at the bag she was filling. "Because. I'm going to move out. This marriage was a mistake."

The panic gave way to a bone-deep fear. And an equally deep anger. "A mistake? What the hell is wrong with you? You've been acting weird for weeks, and then I get a call from Mort Brockhiser telling me you walked out in the middle of your appointment and he was worried you had gotten ill."

"Ah. Mr. Brockhiser. Your *good friend.*" Her voice began to heat around the edges. "Your good friend the banker mentioned today that you'd offered to back up my loan application."

"I—what?" He was taken aback. "That's not right. I *never*—"

"He told me," she said heatedly. "So don't bother denying it."

"I *am* denying it!" Ryan fell silent, his mind reviewing every scrap of his chance encounter with Brockhiser. He'd never…then his own words came floating back into his mind. What had he said? That he'd back anything she attempted? Hell, he hadn't meant it literally. "Uh, I think you—and Mort—misunderstood what I said." He strove for a calmer tone.

"It doesn't matter." She dismissed his overture with one crushing line.

"It matters to *me*. I told him if I were a banker I'd back anything you chose to try, because I believe in you," he said stiffly. "*Not* because I intended to throw money at a bad risk."

"It's not a bad risk."

"I *know* that!" he roared. "Didn't I just say so?"

Jessie sank to the edge of the bed, massaging her back and sighing. "Look, Ryan, I'm sorry if I worried you. If I misunderstood anything, I'll apologize for that, too—"

"You did."

"But this—" she gestured absently around the room "—isn't going to work."

"What isn't going to work?" He was afraid he knew what she meant, but he didn't want to hear it, didn't want to believe it.

"Our marriage."

"Why?"

"You only married me to get children!" she shouted.

"And you married me for the same reason!" he shot back, goaded beyond endurance.

There was a shocked silence in the room as the harsh words ricocheted over and over in the sullen atmosphere.

"And, of course, for my money," he added bitterly.

"For your *money?*" She sucked in a deep breath, and her voice was outraged. "If I wanted your money so badly, then why am I so upset about you horning in on my loan?"

The question hammered at his mind for a moment, but he recovered swiftly. "Oh, I guess the room-by-room lists of valuables were just for fun."

She stared at him blankly. Then her gaze sharpened. She stood and walked to her dresser, yanking open the top drawer and withdrawing the rest of the papers he'd found that day, tossing them wildly into the air, where they fluttered accusingly to the carpet. "If you're talking about these, 'just for fun' is exactly what they were. Something to keep my mind off the fact that I was going stark raving mad lying here incubating. And if you don't believe me, you can ask Finn. It was his suggestion."

Her face was paper white now, and her hands were

shaking as she turned away from him and picked up the sweater she'd discarded, tossing it in the suitcase without folding it. The small gesture was a measure of how truly upset she was, since the Jessie he knew wouldn't even toss *dirty* clothes in a basket without folding them first.

"Jess," he said quietly. Desperately. "I don't want you to go."

"I have to," she replied equally quietly.

"Where? Where will you go?" Suddenly he was fighting for his marriage, his very *life*.

"I'm staying at the Hilton over near the Hynes Convention Center for three days. Then I'll be moving back into my condo."

He was stunned. "Your condo? I thought the lease was up at the end of this month."

"I renewed it," she said tonelessly.

I renewed it. The words were meaningless for a moment. Then, as he absorbed the blow, every ounce of hope drained out of him. She hadn't just made that decision today—she'd only left the bank two hours ago. Which meant… "You never intended to stay married to me, did you?" he said, swallowing the pain that rose in intense waves to pummel his heart. "This was some temporary measure…for what? If it wasn't the money, then *why?*"

She sat down again carefully, holding her hands under the bulk of their babies as if the extra weight hurt. "I thought it would work." For the first time she looked fully at him, and there was a wealth of suffering in her eyes. "We had friendship—and I was pretty sure we would have passion, like you said—but I can't live my life like this, Ryan." She stood and walked awkwardly to the window, and her fingers were white on the sill. "It's not enough. I never expected to have a real marriage and a real family, but you made me want it all—" She shook her head blindly, then threw it back to stare at the ceiling, and he could hear tears in her voice. "I can't compete with a ghost. I'll never be Wendy. And if you ever meet someone who can give you what you had with her, I don't want to be around to watch. To be in the way. It would hurt too much."

Dear God. Was she saying what he thought—hoped, prayed—she was saying? He started forward. "Jess—"

"No." She flung out an arm, and he stopped. "Don't. We'll share the children, I promise you that. I won't move away and I won't deny you equal time. You'll be able to—"

"Jessie!" He was nearly shouting. Again. Two strides brought him to her side, his heart beating a frantic rhythm in his chest. His fingers trembled as he reached for her shoulders and gently turned her around.

She was crying. It hurt him to see her tears, but hope and happiness were rising so rapidly he couldn't focus on the pain. "Jess…are you saying…" He took a deep breath, knowing that if he were wrong, if he'd misunderstood her, his life as he knew it, *needed it to be,* would be over. He tried again. "Do you love me?"

Her eyes were deep, emerald pools, shimmering with tears that seemed to double their pace as they rolled down her face. She nodded.

She nodded! He exhaled without even realizing he'd been holding his breath. "Do you know," he said carefully, his hands sliding down from her shoulders to grip her upper arms lightly, "how long I've loved you? How many years I've wanted you?"

She stared up at him, mesmerized by the intensity of his blue eyes as he held her gaze. She swallowed. "You…you love me?"

He shook her the tiniest bit, very lightly. "I love you. I've loved you for*ever*."

She couldn't take it in. "But, you never told me—"

"You never seemed interested in hearing it." His voice was soft, and echoes of old hurts vibrated.

She remembered other times when they'd skirted the edges of the past. Carefully, afraid to believe it, she said, "But when I came back to Boston you already were married. I was…so shocked. And…hurt, too."

His face grew even more sober. "I gave up. When you went south, I knew I didn't have a chance. Then Wendy came along—"

"Don't." Quickly she reached up and placed her palm across his lips. "I understand. I don't ever expect to take her place."

"No," he agreed. "You can never take her place."

The words twisted like a knife deep in a wound, and she grimaced, lowering her head to hide her expression from him. *You can deal with it,* she thought to herself. *He said he loves you, too.*

"But that's because you owned the largest piece of my heart long before I ever met Wendy." His voice dropped. "I *did* love her, but there was a part of me that always recognized—and regretted—that she wasn't you."

Shock rippled through her and she sagged in his grip.

He made a sound of alarm, then maneuvered her to the edge of the bed, lowering himself to sit beside her with one heavy arm around her back. "Are you all right?"

She nodded. Then she raised a palm to the side of his face, closing her eyes briefly in pleasure at the feel of his warm, beard-stubbled jaw beneath her hand. "All these months," she whispered, "I wanted you to love *me*. And now…you do." She shook her head. "Pinch me. This is a dream."

Ryan chuckled, the sound filled with relief. "I can think of a lot of things I'd like to do to you, but pinching you isn't on the list." He turned his face into her hand, pressing a slow kiss into the softness of her palm. "God, I love you. I've loved you forever, it seems." He raised his gaze to hers. "Tell me."

"I love you." Her words were low and intense, and she leaned forward, inviting him to set his mouth on hers.

He gathered her closer, one arm around her, the other resting on her bulging belly. Gently, tenderly, he took her mouth in a kiss so sweet she felt more tears rising. "I have got to be the luckiest guy in the world."

"And I'm the luckiest woman," she added.

"Does this mean you'll reconsider moving out?"

Her face fell as she remembered his reaction to her lease renewal. "I'm sorry I didn't trust you. I guess…it's hard for me to let go of my independence."

"Because you've never been able to depend on anyone else," he said. "But I promise you that I will always be here, for whatever you need. If you don't want my money, that's fine. If you want it all, that's fine, too. We're one now, in all the ways that count."

And she felt the same way. Once she'd feared commitment, her fear buried deep down in a place she hadn't even been able to acknowledge. She'd been afraid that letting herself love would open her up to more of the heartache she'd experienced as a child, when she'd longed for love from people who didn't have it to give. And because they hadn't, she'd told herself it was better to live without it.

She smiled, tracing his lips with a tender finger. "Actually, we'll soon be *four*. Isn't that a scary thought?"

He shook his head. "Not in the least. Not when I know I'll be sharing the future with you."

Epilogue

"Catch, Daddy!"

Ryan put up a hand almost reflexively as a surprisingly well-aimed baseball came flying straight at his chest the moment he stepped out of the garage. "Hey!" he said, wincing as the ball stung his bare palm. "Wait until I change clothes and get a glove, okay, Liv?"

Olivia Shaughnessy spit elaborately onto the ground as only a four-year-old could and came swaggering toward her father. "Okay."

"Where's your sister?" Ryan scooped his eldest terror up in one arm and nuzzled her neck as she shrieked.

A window opened on the second floor. "Olivia!" Jessie's dark head emerged. "I just got Tyler to sleep, and if you wake him, I swear I'll serve you for dinner. Oh, hi!" Her face lit up as she saw that her husband was home. "Be right down." And she vanished.

"Lanie's helpin' Finn paint Matthew's room," Livvie informed her father. "I was, too, but I got tired of painting."

"I see." As the back door opened, he glanced over his daughter's shining copper curls, drinking in the sight of his wife standing on the stoop. She held a struggling tot on her hip, and she blew her hair out of her eyes with pursed lips as she smiled at Ryan.

"Look, Mattie! Daddy's home." The little boy squirmed down and raced over to attach himself to Ryan's kneecap.

"Hi, squirt." Ryan scooped up his nearly three-year-old son in his free arm and kissed him noisily, noticing splatters of blue paint liberally applied to the little hands. "Were you helping Finn, too?"

"Uh-huh." Matthew held up his hands and regarded them, frowning. "Dirty."

"Yeah." Ryan squatted and set both children down. "Why don't you guys go in and tell Finn it's quitting time. Then wash your hands and get ready for dinner."

He stood, smiling as they raced off, and opened his arms. Jessie came into them, sliding her hands around his waist and up his back beneath his summer suitcoat. "Hi, handsome."

His heart skipped a beat at the warm, loving glow in her eyes. Dropping his head, he sought her mouth, enjoying the feel of her still-slim curves pressed against him. Would he ever get used to being loved by her? Even now, after five years and four children, she still had the power to turn his knees to jelly when she smiled. Her love was a miracle in his life.

"How was your day?" he asked. "Tyler still so bent out of shape?" Their youngest son would be six months old tomorrow and he was teething. Last night they had taken turns walking the fussing baby.

"Not so bad." She pressed a kiss to the side of his neck, speaking against his skin. "That tooth is finally through. He took good naps today, and I bet he'll sleep better tonight."

A shiver of sexual pleasure ran down his spine at the feel of her soft, open mouth on him, and he ran his hands down her back to cup the warm curves of her bottom. "I hope so. I have big plans for tonight."

She laughed, pressing herself closer against the unmistakable evidence of his "plans." "You certainly do," she murmured.

"Only if you're not too tired, though." Although his need for her was as strong as it had been the day they'd first made love, he knew that overseeing four children and a thriving business, even with the help of Finn and Penny, could be exhausting. The nights when he did nothing more than hold her in his arms were as sweet as the nights when they wrecked the bed, simply because there was no one else in the world with whom he'd rather spend his life.

"I got a nap today," she said, unaware of the direction of his thoughts.

"Good." He kissed her again, lingering over her, leisurely drawing her tongue into his mouth and tenderly exploring hers as he drew her closer against him. "I love you," he whispered against her lips. "The day you decided you wanted to have a baby was the luckiest day of my life."

"The day I decided it should be fathered by an 'eminently available hunk' was mine," she said, her eyes dancing as he picked her up and carried her into the home that rang with the joyous sounds of the family they'd created together.

* * * * *

Look for
BILLIONAIRE BACHELORS: STONE,
Anne Marie Winston's next
Silhouette Desire,
in March 2002.

January 2002
THE REDEMPTION OF JEFFERSON CADE
#1411 by BJ James

M E N
of
Belle Terre

Don't miss the fifth book in BJ James' exciting miniseries featuring irresistible heroes from Belle Terre, South Carolina.

February 2002
THE PLAYBOY SHEIKH
#1417 by Alexandra Sellers

SONS OF THE **DESERT**

Alexandra Sellers continues her sensual miniseries about powerful sheikhs and the women they're destined to love.

March 2002
BILLIONAIRE BACHELORS: STONE
#1423 by Anne Marie Winston

Bestselling author Anne Marie Winston's Billionaire Bachelors prove they're not immune to the power of love.

MAN OF THE MONTH

Some men are made for lovin'—and you're sure to love these three upcoming men of the month!

Available at your favorite retail outlet.

Silhouette®
Where love comes alive™

Visit Silhouette at www.eHarlequin.com

SDMOM02Q1

Bestselling author
CAIT LONDON
**brings you another captivating book
in her unforgettable miniseries**

*One Western family finds the love that
legends—and little ones—are made of.*

Available in February 2002:
TALLCHIEF: THE HUNTER
Silhouette Desire #1419

Return to Tallchief Mountain as Adam Tallchief claims his
heritage and the woman he is destined to love. After twenty-
two years, Adam has come home to the family he didn't
know he has. But his old love and enemy, Jillian Green O'Malley,
is back, as well, and the passion that has always blazed
between them threatens to consume them both....

"Cait London is an irresistible storyteller."
—Romantic Times Magazine

Available at your favorite retail outlet.

Where love comes alive™

Silhouette®

where love comes alive—online...

SINTL1R2

You are invited to enter the exclusive, masculine world of the...

TEXAS Cattleman's Club
The Last Bachelor!

Silhouette Desire's powerful miniseries features five wealthy Texas bachelors—all members of the state's most prestigious club—who set out to uncover a traitor in their midst... and discover their true loves!

THE MILLIONAIRE'S PREGNANT BRIDE
by Dixie Browning
February 2002 (SD #1420)

HER LONE STAR PROTECTOR
by Peggy Moreland
March 2002 (SD #1426)

TALL, DARK...AND FRAMED?
by Cathleen Galitz
April 2002 (SD #1433)

THE PLAYBOY MEETS HIS MATCH
by Sara Orwig
May 2002 (SD #1438)

THE BACHELOR TAKES A WIFE
by Jackie Merritt
June 2002 (SD #1444)

Available at your favorite retail outlet.

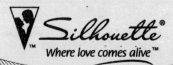

Silhouette®
Where love comes alive™

If you enjoyed what you just read,
then we've got an offer you can't resist!

Take 2 bestselling
love stories FREE!
Plus get a FREE surprise gift!

Clip this page and mail it to Silhouette Reader Service™

IN U.S.A.
3010 Walden Ave.
P.O. Box 1867
Buffalo, N.Y. 14240-1867

IN CANADA
P.O. Box 609
Fort Erie, Ontario
L2A 5X3

YES! Please send me 2 free Silhouette Desire® novels and my free surprise gift. After receiving them, if I don't wish to receive anymore, I can return the shipping statement marked cancel. If I don't cancel, I will receive 6 brand-new novels every month, before they're available in stores! In the U.S.A., bill me at the bargain price of $3.34 plus 25¢ shipping and handling per book and applicable sales tax, if any*. In Canada, bill me at the bargain price of $3.74 plus 25¢ shipping and handling per book and applicable taxes**. That's the complete price and a savings of at least 10% off the cover prices—what a great deal! I understand that accepting the 2 free books and gift places me under no obligation ever to buy any books. I can always return a shipment and cancel at any time. Even if I never buy another book from Silhouette, the 2 free books and gift are mine to keep forever.

225 SEN DFNS
326 SEN DFNT

Name	(PLEASE PRINT)	
Address	Apt.#	
City	State/Prov.	Zip/Postal Code

* Terms and prices subject to change without notice. Sales tax applicable in N.Y.
** Canadian residents will be charged applicable provincial taxes and GST.
  All orders subject to approval. Offer limited to one per household and not valid to
  current Silhouette Desire® subscribers.
  ® are registered trademarks of Harlequin Enterprises Limited.

DES01   ©1998 Harlequin Enterprises Limited